The Road To Power

I0551638

Sanne Wijker

2018 Sveko publishing

All rights reserved © 2018 by Sanne Wijker

Cover design and layout Kors Wijker

Sveko publishing

ISBN/EAN 978-90-819613-2-5

The Road To Power

Just a fantasy story, written for entertainment only.

Any similarity to real individuals or events is purely accidental in nature.

Ambition is a good servant but a bad master.

Uknown.

Table of Contents

Part 1

A STRANGER IN A STRANGE COUNTRY

Part 2.

THE QUEEN OF ELVES

Part 3.

THE CURSE OF THE DRAKEVUURS.

Part I

A STRANGER IN A STRANGE COUNTRY

Place: The Tarnian Autonomy. Time: Some 10 years before the year '16

Chapter 1. Walter Goes on Vacation

Walter Raff rather enjoyed his vacation. It was only two weeks long and he was determined to get the most out of it. It was very unfortunate that he had to spend the greatest part of his life in town and leave Millie, his sister, virtually alone since Aunt Leticia wasn't really much of a company.

Millie was an eager, active type of girl, thoroughly frustrated by her aunt's attempts to turn her into a homebody like herself, only interested in tea and gossip. It was quite natural for a healthy girl of 19 to wish to see more of life than staying in a dreary small village allowed. Yet there was nothing Walter could do about it since he couldn't offer her a proper home himself.

He realized only too well that a big city like Stentis had too many temptations for someone with Millie's disposition and he didn't have time to play her chaperone. He tried to spend as much time with his sister as possible and take her out more. Millie had been thrilled at the prospect of mountain-climbing with the brother whom she adored so mountain-climbing they went.

She looked extremely cute in her sturdy boots, black leggings and rather short denim skirt which Aunt Leticia found positively scandalous.

"What is this world coming to," she would say with a sigh, "if a girl of your age spends time running around in the state of undress instead of sitting home and cross-stitching?"

"Well, it's full 4 inches below the knee," Millie had protested, "and you couldn't expect me to wear a longer skirt now, could you? It would be dangerous in the mountains."

"Child, you are not supposed to go into the mountains at all!" said Aunt Leticia stubbornly. "And so close to the border, too! With all these…things going on in Tarna, it's hardly reasonable."

"We aren't going to cross over, thank you very much," he had said, trying to calm his aunt. "Whatever is going on in Tarna, it stays on their side and we stay on ours."

Tarnian politics were a constant source of irritation to his aunt, whose patriotism made her spend a considerable amount of time every day denouncing the evils of foreign occupation and praising the virtues of those who fought against it. The leaders of the autonomy didn't do enough, in her opinion, to support the true patriots in their fight against Uranians who were synonymous with the Devil in her vocabulary. In fact, the outrageousness of the foreign power occupying the biggest part of the territory of their planet was probably the only subject the aunt and niece ever agreed upon.

Walter had sincerely tried to warn his sister about the dangers of getting involved in Tarnian politics, but was far from sure he had succeeded. Not with Aunt Leticia counteracting his influence day by day.

"Well," he thought now, "this vacation will do her a lot of good. And luckily, there are no known rebel supporters in our village so there is little chance that Millie ever gets in touch with one."

He then remembered the stories he had heard about Doctor Grant, but dismissed them as country gossip. Anyway, the sun was shining, melting the snow on the tops of the nearby mountains. It was spring on Tarna and the weather had been exceptionally good so far.

"Today we are going to climb the Black Crow," he said, pointing the direction to Millie. His sister had auburn hair, just like himself, but his eyes were brown while hers were gray. She was slender and rather tall for a girl but Walter with his 1. 90m towered over her. He was 7 years older, too.

"Look, Millie," he continued, "do you see this peak behind the Black Crow? That's already the territory of Tarna. There is a famous pass over there, but we aren't going that far. We will stay on the side of the autonomy. The Black Crow is a tourist attraction. It's 1050m high and there is a hut on top of it, for those who wish to spend a night there, but I don't think we'll stay so late, I suggest we drive half way up and then get further on foot. In that manner we can manage it all in one day. You know your aunt will get a fit if you spend a night on a mountain top, even if it's in your brother's company."

Millie giggled. "Auntie Leticia is a darling," she said, "but so old-fashioned, isn't she now?"

They followed his plan, driving along a serpentine road which at times went as steep as the angle of 20%, so that it was a real challenge to drive. Walter breathed a sigh of relief when they finally left the car behind in the parking place. It was still early in the morning and as he could see they were the only tourists so far.

He calculated that it would take them about two hours to climb the rest of the distance so that they could eat their lunch on top of the Black Crow. He had climbed it once before with a group of friends and the view was breath-taking.

It was about midday and both brother and sister were quite tired when they finally reached the top. The hut was still standing there and close to it, a bench where one could sit and enjoy the view. Walter sank upon it rather contentedly, but Millie, who seemed to have acquired the second breath once they reached their destination, was eager to explore.

She declared she was going inside the hut first, to inspect. Walter pointed out that there wasn't really much to inspect, but she ran off before he could finish the sentence. She disappeared inside and a couple of seconds later he heard her scream. Walter jumped to his feet and saw his sister standing in the entrance of the hut, looking very pale.

"Walter," she said, stammering. "The-the-there is a man in there. A dead man."

Chapter 2. A Difficult Choice

"He isn't dead," said Walter. He was kneeling beside the stranger on the wooden floor of the mountain hut. It was a man of about his own age or a couple of years older, with raven-black hair. Dressed as a tourist, he was lying face down in the pool of his own blood. But he was not dead, at least, not yet.

Walter carefully turned the wounded man around. He had regular features and was of a type a girl like Millie would find handsome. Walter tried to determine the nature of the stranger's injuries. His jacket had a hole on the right side definitely caused by a ray gun shot and that was apparently where all the blood had come from, but he wasn't bleeding any more.

The man's face was deathly pale but he was still breathing. Walter took out his knife and cut through the jacket. There was a scarf pressed under it, soaking wet, as the stranger evidently had tried to stop the bleeding. It was placed under the shoulder on the right side of his chest and Walter's admittedly restricted medical knowledge told him that the wound was probably not lethal. There was no bloody foam on the man's lips so that the lung wasn't damaged, either.

"Look," said Millie suddenly in a coarse voice. "There, in the corner."

A ray gun was lying where the stranger apparently had dropped it when he collapsed on the floor. Walter whistled. "This is the matter for the police," he said, reaching for his mobile.

Millie grabbed his hand. "Don't," she said. "They'll send him back and you know what it means."

"It's none of our business," retorted Walter. "And, besides, what do you suggest that we do? Illegal border-crossing is a serious offence."

"Let's look if he has any documents first," pleaded Millie.

Walter felt rather uncomfortable searching through the stranger's pockets but he was relieved when he finally found a passport in one of them. A Tarnian passport.

"Well, he won't go far with this," he said, showing it to Millie. "A Tarnian passport and a hole in his chest is evidence enough. There is probably a price on his head, too."

As he was speaking, the man on the floor opened his eyes and looked around, then muttered something incomprehensible and appeared to have lost his consciousness again.

"We can't abandon him to his fate," urged Millie.

"Shall we take him home then?" asked Walter ironically. "Millie, you don't know what you are talking about."

"I'm ashamed of you!" exclaimed his sister stomping her foot. "Walter, how can you? It's bad enough that our cowardly authorities deport all those trying to escape, they surely don't need our help to do evil."

"Evil is a big word," responded Walter calmly. "Really, Millie, you know perfectly well that our small army isn't a match for the Uranians, if we don't comply with their demands we'll simply share the fate of the rest of Tarna. Be glad we are still free to live the way we do. But you are right; we can't just leave him lying like this. Here, give me a hand."

Millie smiled triumphantly. She knew her brother well enough, once he got involved in something, he'd stick with it to the end. She held the stranger's head as Walter poured some water out of the plastic bottle onto his face and tried to make him drink. It helped and the injured man opened his eyes again.

"Who are you?" he asked, to their great surprise speaking in Westen, the common tongue of the Galactical Sector X.

"We are friends," Walter reassured him. "Please stay quiet, it might be dangerous for you to talk. We'll try to help you."

The man nodded and closed his eyes again. He was obviously exhausted. Fighting against nausea, Walter removed the bloody scarf, took his own and that of Millie; then, adding to all this the stripes he had cut out of the stranger's jacket, with his sister's help bound the wound as well as he could. The man was moaning quietly but didn't open his eyes.

After they have finished, Walter looked around. There was blood on the floor and no way to remove it, plus they had the stranger's scarf to dispose of. This and a long way down to where their car was parked which Walter was not at all sure the stranger ever could walk in his condition. And yet they had to leave and quickly. He took a decision and searched the plastic bag they had taken with them fishing out a sandwich. Once he had decided upon a course of action he was always efficient and to the point.

"Millie," he ordered, "stay here and try to make him eat something and drink more water. Don't let him talk, it's too exhausting. I'm going to get the car, it'll take me less than an hour if I go alone, and you can drive nearly to the top of the mountain. The rest of the distance he can walk, I presume, or I'll have to carry him but it's only 200 or 300m. We'll take him back to Cramford and then…then we'll see."

Chapter 3. Back in Cramford

When Walter later looked back at the events of that day they always acquired a nightmarish quality in his mind. The mad descending along the steep road back to the parking place, with his heart pounding as all sorts of unpleasant thoughts were racing through his brain. What if the police arrive before him? After all, they have helicopters. And what if it's not police, but even worse, the Tarnian border guards? They were rather notorious for disregarding the autonomy's laws and crossing over to hunt fugitives.

What if the man dies? What to do with his scarf? Burn it? Throw it away? Take it home and try to wash it out? And the ray gun? What will Aunt Leticia say when she comes back home in three days, after visiting her cousin and finds out they are using her house as a hiding place for an escaped Tarnian rebel? A real one and not one of those she heard about on TV?

Here his thoughts took another turn. If the man was a Tarnian, why was he speaking Westen? It was rather strange. Very strange. Maybe, he wasn't a Tarnian after all. A foreign agent? Tarna was flooded with them lately. That was even worse, for all Walter knew. But he also knew that his sister was right and they could not leave a wounded man to his fate which undoubtedly would be a grim one.

He practically ran all the way down and covered the distance in record time and as for his getting to the top of that mountain, he could have won a prize in dangerous driving had it existed, though luckily for him, the higher you got the less steep the road became.

When he came back, he encountered his sister sitting on the floor with the stranger's head in her lap and he was drinking water out of the bottle. Walter swore under his breath. There was another danger he had forgotten about. Millie with all her stupid romantic ideas inherited from her aunt was an easy prey for an adventurer, especially as handsome as that one.

Walter comforted himself with a thought that the stranger could hardly stay long with them. Douglas Wray, that's what his name was according to his passport. Walter doubted it was his real name though, but anyway, you had to address him somehow.

"Eh, Mr. Wray, can you walk?" asked Walter. The man turned his head slightly and stared. His eyes were green as the sea.

"Mr. Wray?" he repeated, surprised, and then as if recollecting something, continued: "Yes, that's what they call me."

"He is delirious", thought Walter. He repeated his question: "Can you walk?"

"I'll try", said Wray. "After all, I climbed all the way here, didn't I?" He relapsed and fell silent again.

Walk he did, with their mutual help, but when they finally reached the car he fell on the back seat and lay there with his eyes closed. Walter put his ray gun into one of Wray's pockets, and deciding after some consideration that it was better to leave nothing behind used the empty plastic bag in which they had carried their lunch (Millie informed him that she had shared the sandwiches with the stranger who ate one of them) to conceal the bloodied scarf.

They drove back home to Cramford without any problem though once they saw a helicopter flying somewhere in the distance. With Aunt Leticia absent and the housekeeper having taken a week's vacation they had the whole house at their disposal.

The most important thing right now was to smuggle the stranger inside without the neighbors noticing. Luckily, their aunt's house was situated on the outskirts of the village and had an ample back garden close to the mountain slope with a big shed and a private parking lot.

"We'll give him my room," said Walter. "It's a temporary arrangement anyway, but my bedroom has an adjacent bathroom. You'll have to take your aunt's room and I'll stay in yours."

While they were discussing these things on the way home, Wray took no part in their conversation whatsoever. He was lying there so quietly that Walter felt uneasy for a moment. What if he really would die? However, the stranger was still alive when they finally arrived and Walter parked the car, and he even managed to walk as far as the door wearing Walter's jacket on his shoulders for camouflage. Walter had admired the stranger's determination but the attempt to climb the stairs proved too much for Wray so that he was obliged to carry their new acquaintance all the way upstairs and lay him in bed.

"Well, this part of our plan has succeeded," he said, wiping his forehead. "Now, what are we going to do next?"

"Why, call Dr. Grant, of course!" answered Millie cheerfully.

Chapter 4. A Deltan Agent?

"He was tortured," said Dr. Grant, addressing Walter as they were in the room together. "Look at this."

Dr. Grant was a man in his fifties with graying hair and piercing blue eyes. He didn't appear particularly surprised when, after Walter had called him and asked to visit them on the account of his sister's bad headache, he encountered a wounded Tarnian rebel in Walter's bed instead.

"You did a good thing in calling me, Walter," was the only thing he said. "And it's a good thing I always carry my medical bag with me wherever I go."

Together they partially removed the stranger's clothes. His wound wasn't particularly dangerous, just as Walter had thought, but he had lost a lot of blood.

"He really needs a transfusion," remarked Dr. Grant, "and a couple of days in a good hospital, but since he's young and apparently, overall healthy, he should be getting better in a couple of days. A tetanus shot, antibiotics and some morphine will do the trick. Now, if you hold him up like this, I'll put on a bandage."

It was at that moment that the doctor had a good chance to have a look at the stranger's back and he uttered an exclamation of surprise and dismay. Walter looked, too, and discovered several dark stripes which had all the appearance of having been the result of a severe whipping.

"His hands also," said Dr. Grant, pointing to the lines on the man's wrists. "They'd probably let him hang like this for a couple of days. He must possess some important information."

In a flash of inspiration he removed Wray's socks and they both saw an old scar on one of his ankles.

"And he's been a part of a chain gang, too," summed up Walter somberly.

"What are we going to do about all this?" he asked half an hour later while Douglas Wray was sleeping as peacefully as the morphine shot would allow.

Dr. Grant was deep in thought and appeared not to hear him at first, then started and looked at Walter.

"Well, to begin with, we have to find out his true identity. Of course, he can't stay here long, it's too dangerous. Come, let's go downstairs and listen to the 6 o'clock news, maybe we'll learn something."

They learned something all right. It was all over the news that a group of dangerous terrorists tried to cross the border last night. Two of them were killed by the Tarnian border guards but an especially dangerous one managed to escape. He was wounded and probably not able to go far. His name was Douglas Wray, he was 28 years old, 1.80m high, short black hair, green eyes, wanted alive and the authorities of Tarna would pay 10 000 pounds to anyone who helped them to arrest him. Furthermore, they had to remind their viewers that harboring fugitives was a federal crime which carried with itself a penalty of a heavy fine and up to 5 years in prison etc. etc.

Grant and Walter looked at each other. "It couldn't be much worse," said Walter gloomily, "could it now, Doctor?"

Dr. Grant was pondering the situation and didn't answer so that Walter went on. "And I can bet Wray isn't his real name, either. He spoke Westen to us when he first came by. Why do they want him so much? Why did they torture him? There must be a reason for all this."

"He may be a Deltan agent," suggested Grant. "That would explain a lot of things. In this case it's our duty to give Wray all the assistance possible since Deltans are the only people in the whole Galaxy who care about Tarna and try to help us."

"How are we supposed to do it?" inquired Walter. "It probably won't take them long to trace him here, either. My aunt's returning in a couple of days. And the housekeeper. Neither of these women could keep their mouths shut if their lives depended on it."

"I know, old boy, I know. I'll do my best to arrange something. In the meanwhile try to impress the necessity of holding her tongue on your sister, will you?"

Chapter 5. Eric Looks Back

Eric opened his eyes in a strange room. It took him some time to recollect how he got there. His thoughts were blurred. He could remember their last desperate climb and the ambush, the fight, Harry dying and himself and Brad managing to escape. He knew he had been wounded. He had pressed his scarf against the wound trying to stop the bleeding. There were already on the territory of the Tarnian autonomy and the guards stopped their pursuit.

Brad collapsing to the ground, with bloody foam on his lips. His last words, urging him to get on. He had to deliver the message. The rest of his way Eric couldn't remember at all. The mist in front of his eyes was getting thicker the higher he climbed. Then he saw the hut and an animal instinct drove him into it. And then, what happened then?

Somebody must have found him and brought here. Where? There was a woman's voice, and there was a man or were it two men? Eric didn't know. All he knew was that it felt like real luxury to lie in a normal bed again after camping in the mountains for several weeks.

For some time, he was just enjoying the feeling but then the more pressing problem engrossed his thoughts. He was being hunted and he couldn't afford to stay in bed, no, not even for one day. He had to keep on going if he wanted to live. And he was intent on staying alive, if only to kill Alec Randall.

In fact, the desire to see Randall dead was probably what had brought him so far. He'd kill him even if it were the last thing he ever did. Randall had been an evil genius of his life, but now he had an upper hand. If only he could manage to leave Tarna. If only he could find a way to deliver the message.

Eric closed his eyes again and thought of the first time he met Alec Randall. It had been nearly two years before and it happened on a beautiful sunny day in a park in the center of the city of Aargh. This park had always been his favorite. That day Eric came there, too, and he was sitting on a bench staring at a small artificial pond in front of him with some local birds swimming around happily.

A sort of a duck they were, brightly colored as most tropical birds. Eric followed their movements with his eyes and thought that it was probably the last time he could enjoy the view. He was only 26 and his life was finished. He needed 30 000 Reall next Wednesday and if he didn't pay his debt he'd be sold as a slave.

There was no way he could raise this amount of money in a week's time. Eric had tried to ask his uncle who he was working for to forward him a part of the sum he was due next month for the project he had developed but his uncle flat out refused. They could never stand each other. Steven Ericsson, his father's younger brother, had been forced to leave his native planet many years before and found his second home on Aargh where he engaged in a series of shady businesses including a construction firm where Eric worked as an architect.

His uncle underpaid him and in general, treated him miserably but Eric endured it all simply because he had nowhere else to go. And then he discovered the stock exchange and started his investing career. He became wealthy and could afford a lot of nice things and then he met Irene Stedler. It wasn't love at the first sight. In fact, it wasn't love at all. He had no illusions about Irene from the very beginning and he knew her price was high, but he had desired her and he got her.

She left an incredibly rich merchant in diamonds to stay with him and Eric, who couldn't compete with the latter in the money department but was young and handsome, secretly hoped that she cared for him personally and not only for his money, even though he didn't really love her. For Irene had an expensive taste and made him live above his income.

Eric started taking more and more risks in his speculations and then he lost. He borrowed some money and lost again. And again. And now he had nowhere to go any more. His uncle had been his last hope and he refused.

Eric was a son of an earl. He couldn't imagine a bigger humiliation than to be sold like cattle for his debts which was a normal practice on Aargh. It was better to put an end to it and soon. That was the real reason he had come to the park. He took a ray gun out of his pocket and stared at it. Had it really come to that? Was there no other way?

At that moment, he heard a noise behind his back and a polite voice asked: "Mr. Ericsson, if I'm not mistaken? I need to talk to you."

And that's how he first made acquaintance with Alec Randall.

Chapter 6. How It All Began

Alec Randall didn't waste time beating around the bush. He admitted that he had been following Eric and his activities for quite some time now and that he knew all sorts of things about the latter, including his financial troubles.

He offered to pay his debts if only Eric would agree to do little things for him, such as copying certain documents he handled while functioning as his uncle's personal secretary, delivering parcels to some guests he met during receptions in certain houses he visited, undertaking short trips on behalf of his new employer, gathering information about new building projects the government of Aargh was planning, including the construction of Arshan Dam, these sorts of things.

Eric wasn't naive. He directly asked Randall who he really would be working for, though he knew the answer.

"Does it really matter?" asked the latter and Eric said that yes, it did, to him. He wouldn't be working for Uranians for all the money in the world. Alec Randall smiled. He had a long knife scar on his cheek, dark hair and light blue steely eyes and he was dressed as any successful businessman would be. Eric estimated that he was several years older than himself. He had heard vague hints about him before and he knew that Alec Randall was a very dangerous man.

"I appreciate your patriotism, Mr. Ericsson," said Alec smiling. "You don't have to worry about betraying your principles. You'll be working for one of your home planet's staunch allies, the King of Delta. Now, do you agree?"

Eric did. After all, there was really little else he could do, though he bitterly regretted it afterwards. It was like signing the contract with the Devil. Alec Randall was utterly devoid of any human feelings such as sympathy, mercy or compassion.

He started with informing Eric that any failure to comply with his demands, any information leak would be viewed as treason and handled as such. He drove him to do things Eric regretted including lying, stealing and giving false witness. His uncle, through his dubious connections, was involved in government contracts so that Eric had an access to classified information.

As an architect, he took part in developing some new projects and thus had a perfect opportunity for sabotage which cost several men who Delta wanted to get out of the way their lives. There was an investigation and Eric couldn't sleep at night knowing that if his involvement came out the punishment would be public hanging. They couldn't prove anything and finally came to the conclusion that the mistake lay in the materials used and not in the original design.

Finally, Eric had had enough of it. It was after Roger's death. He never believed it was just an ordinary robbery which left his friend lying in a ditch with two holes in his chest and one in his head. He refused to sign the new contract. Enough was enough, he said. Randall didn't seem to mind, but reappeared a month later, offering him a Deltan passport and enough money to leave Aargh, which Eric hated, and to start a new life on Delta. In exchange, Eric had to go to Tarna disguised as a journalist writing on economic topics, deliver a small parcel and bring back the answer. That was all and it had sounded so simple...

Eric opened his eyes. It was dark outside. How long had he been staying in this house? The door opened and he saw a girl of about 18 come in. She had long curly auburn hair, gray eyes and a pretty smile. Eric recognized her face. This was the girl who had given him water back on the mountain top.

Her smile made him think of someone else, someone he had known in his past life, before he became one of the numerous political refugees on Aargh. Which reminded him again that there was no time to waste. Eric spoke very little Tarnian and hence addressed her in Westen: "Miss, can you tell me where I am?"

Chapter 7. The Hunt Continues

Walter Raff looked at the man lying in his bed. He had dark circles under his eyes and he was running a high fever. Nevertheless, he insisted that he had to leave immediately.

"Mr. Wray, please, keep quiet," he argued. "You can't go anywhere, not in this condition. Now if you stay in bed for a couple of days you are bound to feel better and then you can leave."

He wasn't at all sure that the stranger could comprehend rational arguments, but he had to try anyway. Wray seemed to have changed his mind about getting out of bed. He calmed down and drank the cup of tea Walter had brought him. He was trying to keep his sister out of the way as far as possible, though it was evident to him that Millie was very much in love already.

"Can you tell me what's going on?" inquired Wray. Walter nodded and briefly explained to the stranger how they first found him on top the mountain and how they brought him home that afternoon.

"You are in Cramford now," he continued, "it's a small village about 100 km from the Tarnian border. You are safe while you are staying with us, but you really can't leave until we provide you with new documents and some disguise. You see, they are searching for you, Mr. Wray."

"Just call me Douglas, will you?" answered Eric, remembering that it was the name in his passport which became quite worthless now. Still, it would be better for everyone if his real name weren't mentioned at all.

Walter smiled. "Certainly, eh, Douglas," he said. "And now try to get some sleep. It'll do you a lot of good." He never knew nursing could be so exhausting.

Their visitor's condition improved overnight much more than Walter had dared to hope. In fact, he looked like a different man altogether. There was a color in his cheek and it didn't come from fever, either. Walter tried not to show how relieved he was.

The manhunt was going on and they had shown Wray's picture, too.

Luckily for them all, while the authorities of the autonomy always outwardly complied with the demands of Tarna, in practice they were never too eager to deport anyone and wouldn't look for the fugitives very thoroughly, unless they had a special reason to. Of course, if the police by some chance came across Eric they would arrest him and return to Tarna, and they would probably try to gather information in the nearby villages, but Walter doubted they would do house searches. Not unless someone tipped them off.

Dr. Grant came later in the morning, officially to inquire after Millie's headache. Walter's sister met him enthusiastically.

"So, do you bring any good news today, Doctor?"

Grant smiled. He had always liked Millie. She reminded him of his own daughter who was married and lived in the capital.

"It depends on what you mean by 'good news'," he said. "I came in touch with some friends of mine and they agreed to help. But it means that your new acquaintance will leave you soon, and I'm not sure you'll like it."

"Don't encourage her, Doctor," said Walter, irritated. "It's bad enough without it."

Grant shrugged his shoulders. "It'll go over," he remarked. "Now, how is he today? I want to talk to him alone, if you don't mind."

Walter didn't. He hoped Douglas Wray would leave their house and their life as soon as possible.

"I'm not asking for any details, mind you," said Dr. Grant addressing his new patient. "But if I'm to help, I must know at least something about you and your business here on Tarna. I'm taking risks, too, and my friends as well, as you can understand."

Eric thought a bit. Could the man in front of him be trusted? Could you trust anyone these days? However, he obviously had little choice.

"Douglas Wray is not my real name, as you have probably guessed," he said finally, "but I prefer to use it for now. I arrived from Aargh on business I don't care to talk about and had a chance to enjoy your neighbors' hospitality," he added bitterly, remembering a month he had spent in a Uranian prison.

"By some lucky chance I managed to escape and reach the mountains where I stayed with the rebels for some time, until they provided me and my companion with the new documents and a guide to cross the border. We were ambushed on the way here and both men who had accompanied me were killed. The fact that the authorities know my new name proves, in my opinion, that it was not a coincidence, but rather betrayal; which, I'm told, is a normal occurrence on Tarna these days. There was a price set on my head, you see. I carry an urgent message and wish to leave the planet and return to Aargh as soon as possible. That's all."

Chapter 8. Dr. Grant Has a Plan

"I think it can be arranged, your leaving this planet soon, I mean," said Dr. Grant. "You see, a cousin of my friend is a novice in a monastery not far away from here. They are sending a clerical delegation to Aargh in a week in order to attend a conference on inter-church dialogue. Well, you could be a part of it."

Eric suddenly laughed. "That takes the cake, doesn't it? I mean the religious conference on Aargh. Will they hold it close to the annual slave fair? It starts next week."

"Are you against slavery?" inquired the doctor, curious.

"I'm against Aargh and everything it stands for," replied Eric somberly and thought of a Deltan passport, supposedly awaiting him in the end. He would have never agreed to take any part in another of Alec Randall's crazy schemes had it not been for a chance, however slim it was, to leave the planet where he had spent 5 long years and which he thoroughly hated; for Eric had been born on Dakstra, a Baron Confederation planet which was in all aspects different from Aargh.

Aargh was a place for scoundrels and it acted as a magnet on the worst sort of human trash the Galactical Sector X produced, including his own uncle, but Eric had no choice after he had made an unfortunate decision to fight on the wrong side in a civil war 7 years ago. Granted, at that time he thought it was the right side, but the side that loses is always wrong.

His thoughts returned to his present situation. The idea to leave Tarna disguised as a monk was incredibly amusing. Grant watched Eric's face expression with some alarm and proceeded to ask him whether he belonged to the One True Church.

"I'm afraid I'm what you would call a heretic," Eric informed him, "though my personal beliefs could probably be better described as agnostic. I hope your friend's cousin won't mind."

"I don't think he will," Grant assured him. What he didn't tell Eric was that the person in question, Charlie Stewart, who was one of the gardeners in a big and prosperous Westward Abbey, specialized in producing false documents for Tarnian fugitives and that the Abbey itself was the center of many illegal activities to which the Abbot, who sympathized with the rebels, turned a blind eye, supported in his position by Archbishop Simanis who had personally interfered when the police had once attempted to search the monastery and had threatened every would-be search participant with excommunication. If they could reach the Westward Abbey without any trouble, all Eric's problems would be solved.

"They chose Aargh," explained the doctor, "because of its central position and easy accessibility and because the rent was low."

"Yeah, that's why slave traders love it, too," agreed Eric. "Anyway, how soon can I leave this house?"

"How about this evening?" asked Dr. Grant. "Westward Abbey is 2.5 hours driving from here. I suggest you burn your current passport as you won't be needing it any more. I've already burned your scarf and the remains of your jacket. As for your clothes, we'll have to take that risk as I prefer that you leave nothing behind what could be found and used as evidence against this family. Here is your ray gun, but I sincerely hope you won't get a chance to use it, at least, until you are back on Aargh, that is."

"I sort of missed it," admitted Eric, putting the pistol away. "I was practically sleeping with this thing in my hand for nearly 4 weeks."

"Do you mind telling me how you managed to escape from prison?" inquired Grant.

"I was basically lucky. I always have been," stated Eric. "You see, they were going to transfer me to St. Gottard and that would have undoubtedly been the end of me. There was another prisoner who was also going to be transferred on the same day but several hours later. He appeared to be a university professor and his students organized an escape for him. However, something went wrong and they stopped the van transporting me and by the time they realized their mistake it was already too late to change anything so that they ended up saving me instead of him."

"And what happened to the professor?"

"I'm afraid he was executed a couple of days later, poor devil," said Eric carelessly. "And I'm here, still alive. Isn't it curious how things work out sometimes? The Uranians didn't see any humor in the situation though and took a lot of trouble to ensure that I'd be dead, too. They are a pretty determined bunch, aren't they?"

Dr. Grant nodded. He thought that Eric was perhaps a bit too cynical, but that it was understandable in his situation. "God willing, we'll beat them this time as well," he said aloud, rising up. "Be ready at about half past nine, I'm coming to fetch you. Good-bye for now, Douglas."

Chapter 9. Irene's Secret

Millie had actually tears in her eyes as she was saying good-bye. Eric thought that she was a sweet girl. She had sneaked into his room several times, bringing him a cup of tea, a slice of cake or some chocolates. She also asked all sorts of questions which Eric answered in a very vague manner or didn't answer at all. Still, despite her nosiness, she was a funny child. Quite different from Irene.

As Dr. Grant's car was driving away and Eric stared at the road in front of him he saw something else instead. He saw a big, dimly lit reception room in Countess Elza's house. Of course, he never would have been invited there if not for his uncle. Elza's husband, who was at least 20 years her senior, did business with Steven Ericsson. What sort of business it was Eric didn't know for sure at that time since his uncle never told him everything about his affairs, but he had his suspicions.

Count Marchbold was an extremely wealthy Deltan expat who chose to live on Aargh though he had never bothered to acquire citizenship. However, his wealth was such that he had nothing to fear from the authorities and moved in the first circles. His young wife was very pretty and even more empty-headed and she took a fancy to Eric from the very beginning, which used to drive him mad until he started to see a comical side of this affection.

She would hang on his arm and ask him about his work and the new project he was developing and whether he already found "a good girl" to settle down with, hinting that she probably knew someone just suitable for him. Eric invariably told her that she looked fantastic, that his new project was getting on splendidly and that he wasn't planning to marry in the near future as he was too young.

That didn't discourage the countess in the slightest and she would continue talking in the same manner until another guest arrived who required her attention and that gave Eric the chance to escape. Luckily, Marchbolds' house was always more or less full so she couldn't devote too much time to Eric and his problems.

He didn't quite know himself why he kept visiting there so often, because he was his uncle's secretary and saw it as his duty to accompany him, or because it was the only decent house where he was received. As a penniless political refugee without citizenship (though his uncle bothered to provide him with a legal status) he didn't exactly have a great choice of society.

That evening it was Elza's birthday. She turned 26. She chose to wear a long silvery evening dress with an enormous décolleté showing how well-endowed she was by Nature. The dress didn't suit her well since she was too short and plump to wear something like that and it was certainly too revealing. She was sparkling with diamonds. Her husband dealt in diamonds officially, though Eric was pretty sure he dealt in other things, too; namely, in weapons, drugs and selling secrets.

There was no shady business where money was to be made that the count wouldn't engage in and so did his uncle. That's how it happened that Irene came there, too, with the man she introduced as her cousin but who everybody with half a brain cell immediately understood was her lover. Of course, just like Eric, she wouldn't be received in any other house than this. She looked exceptionally well that evening, with her long dark hair hanging half way down her back and wearing a simple white dress which looked so elegant; especially when one compared her with their overdressed hostess. On her neck she had a thin golden necklace with one big diamond.

Eric was smitten. Of course, he had had other women before as it was impossible to live on Aargh and keep one's innocence, but this was something entirely different. And yet, even at the height of his attraction he never called the feeling which possessed him, love.

He sighed, recollecting how thrilled he had been when she first moved into his tiny, three-room apartment. His uncle was mad. He went as far as to tell his nephew that he was openly disregarding public morals, but Eric only shrugged his shoulders. Public morals on Aargh? And coming from his uncle, it was really rich.

"I don't drag my paramours home," said Steven Ericsson furiously. "That's the difference. As your uncle, I have a duty to warn you. That gold-digger will ruin you. "

In retrospect, he had been right, admitted Eric; but despite everything, they still had had a darn good time together until Irene somehow got an idea that he had to marry her. She realized she was nearing 30 and she wanted to settle down. When she first approached the topic, Eric stared at her incredulously. The idea was preposterous. He could just imagine his father's face when he brought her home.

"Father, this is Irene Stedler, my prospective wife."

"Irene Who?"

Lord Ravencroft never took trouble to control his temper while talking to his youngest son; he always said precisely what he thought of Eric, his friends, his ideas and his way of life.

"Sweetheart, why do you want to get married anyway? Marriage is shackles."

That made her raving mad. "You wouldn't say this if you were addressing your equal!" screamed Irene. She had a piercing voice if she started screaming. "You wouldn't dare to say it to her!"

"To whom?" inquired Eric, surprised.

"To her! That woman you loved on Dakstra! The one you told me about once, when you were drunk, remember? The princess."

Eric swore. Damn it, why couldn't he have held his tongue?

"Of course I wouldn't say it to her. She was not a…"

At that moment she tried to slap him and he had to lock her in the bedroom.

"If you don't stop behaving in that manner," he informed her, "they'll kick us out of this apartment complex. It's supposedly a middle class neighborhood, so they don't approve of gutter rows over here."

It was only their first fight on the matter, many more ensued, but that was not what finally drove them apart. It's only after Eric found out about her involvement with Alec Randall that he finally kicked her out of his house and his life. In fact, he was so mad he wondered why he hadn't killed her...

Chapter 10. More Complications

It was Roger who told him. Roger had been an old pal of his. Eric first met him when the latter interrupted a bar fight in which Eric wasn't exactly on the winning side, and they had been friends ever since. Roger was a Tarnian immigrant with a legal status though his work as a travelling salesman could hardly bring enough money to purchase it.

The source of his wealth had always been a mystery to Eric just as much as his frequent disappearances. Sure, he had to travel for his work, but in Eric's opinion, it was still not a sufficient explanation. It's only after he had signed the contract with Randall that he found out the truth. Roger had been working for Alec as a courier and probably worse than that.

He never talked much about the exact nature of his work but Eric got a distinct impression that Roger knew more than it was good for him. He also had drinking bouts and they were getting worse. It was during one of them, when they both were sitting in the same bar their acquaintance had begun, that he told Eric how he thought his life was in danger.

"I won't get much older, that's for sure," he stated with a strange laugh.

"Nonsense," retorted Eric, but he thought by himself that it probably explained Roger's drinking. His fears were getting the upper hand of him. In fact, it looked as if his friend were on the verge of a nervous breakdown.

Roger was silent for a moment and then asked: "How is Irene?"

"As usual," said Eric. The truth was that they were now having fights every single day. "She'd be much better if she hadn't got that ridiculous idea somehow that I have to marry her."

"Yeah, she's always wanted to marry," agreed Roger. "In fact, she was rather close to the altar before she met you. She's been with you for nearly three years now so if you dump her it'll be darn difficult for her to start all over again. But then she'll have Alec to take care of her."

"Alec?" asked Eric dryly.

"Why, Alec Randall, of course! She was a good acquaintance of his, was she, our Irene." After those words were spoken, Roger fell with his face on the table and Eric wasn't able to get a word out of him anymore.

He went home and confronted Irene. She told him a virtual sob story about Alec helping her when she was left penniless after her parents' death, and how they had been friends ever since. Eric ordered her to pack her things and to get out. Cold fury possessed him when he thought that like a thousand other total idiots before him, he had fallen for a honey trap, and that not even for a woman he really cared about.

Irene sank to her knees and was crying hysterically. She told him she loved him and had nowhere else to go. When later Eric thought about the events of that evening calmly, he had to admit that it looked like a scene out of a bad operetta.

By that time, he had a ray gun in his hand. He informed her that she had exactly 10 minutes to get out of his apartment before he shot her dead. The only thing which really kept him from killing her was a small voice in his head which mockingly asked him if he were actually fool enough to expect loyalty from a prostitute.

"Your fine friend Alec Randall will take care of you!" he said through his teeth. Something in his face convinced Irene he meant it and then she became truly scared. He ended up giving her all the cash he had at home and then she was finally gone.

Next week, Roger was found dead in a ditch in a bad neighborhood, but he managed to send a letter to Eric before his death. A couple of days later, Alec Randall appeared out of nowhere, waving a Deltan passport in front of his nose…

Eric's reflections were interrupted in a very unpleasant manner. While he was thus recollecting the past, Dr. Grant, who was driving, kept listening to the police radio and his face expression got gloomier and gloomier.

By some reason this time, the autonomy authorities really meant business in their quest for the fugitive. The villages were being searched and the highways were closed. The monastery was less than an hour driving from Cramford if one used the main road, but Grant chose narrow country lanes on purpose. He knew that if the police once stopped them, it would be the end of the game.

He first thought of hiding Eric in the trunk, but what was the use of it if they searched all cars? And they did. Twice there was a sound of a helicopter flying above their heads, but both times it disappeared somewhere in the direction of the border. All this activity was rather puzzling when you considered the fact that lots of other unlucky guys crossed the border regularly looking for asylum and there was seldom much fuss about it. But now well.

It could have but one reason only: the man who called himself Douglas Wray was in the possession of some very important information and Uranians, the real rulers of Tarna, were determined not to let him escape. They probably exercised a lot of pressure on the autonomy authorities.

Dr. Grant kept looking in the mirror nervously and when he saw another car going the same direction he felt, at first, uneasiness, then a sinking feeling in his stomach and then certainty. They were being pursued. He pushed the gas pedal into the floor and as the car accelerated, it shook from top to bottom.

Eric awoke from his reverie. Grant was driving as fast as he could on a dangerously narrow road with an abyss on one side of them, but their pursuers were determined to keep up. They now put the siren on and through the megaphone commanded them to stop. Eric's hand went into his pocket.

"Don't, you damn fool!" shouted the doctor. "You are not in mainland Tarna anymore! You can't go around killing people over here!"

At that rather critical moment there was a crashing sound behind them. The driver of the police car lost control over the steering wheel and it first crashed into a low concrete parapet and then went all the way down and fell into the river below. Dr. Grant's mind went totally blank for a moment. He was now responsible for the death of two men.

Eric cursed softly. And then thanked Heaven that Grant had taken the precaution to cover his license plates with mud on both sides. They still had a chance to escape.

Chapter 11. Safe at Last?

They would have probably never reached the Abbey if Dr. Grant hadn't known the area so well. Despite his state of mind, he managed to keep his head cool and making a turn chose another route, over the mountain top. That road was practically deserted as it was hardly used anymore, being much more suited for a horse and a carriage than for a car, at least, in Eric's opinion.

He had felt uncomfortable more than once but they finally made it to the other side of the pass and soon saw the walls of the monastery rising in front of them. The Westward Abbey was very old and its architecture had much of a medieval castle, though behind the walls one could find a modern hotel for tourists and pilgrims and a store which sold everything from religious books and maps of the region to candles, wine and noodles made by monks.

It was past 11 p.m. standard time when they finally arrived, and the doors were closed; but Charlie evidently had been waiting for them. Ancient though the walls might be, the heavy gate was quite modern and operated by remote control, it slid to one side to let them in.

Dr. Grant breathed a sigh of relief as he drove inside and saw his friend's cousin standing in the parking place in his novice habit and waving. Charlie Stewart was 25 and spent the last two years as a junior gardener in the Abbey, at least, officially; unofficially he specialized in making false autonomy passports and had his own small laboratory in one of the wine cellars. Another cellar was used by the rebels to store weapons.

The Abbot didn't mind, with one caveat: the weapons were not to be used on the territory of the Free Republic of Tarna, as the autonomy was officially called. It wasn't evident how much Simanis really knew, for though a staunch patriot, His Excellency had always stressed that he preferred political methods of solving the conflict and disapproved of terrorism.

Dr. Grant opened the window and Charlie enthusiastically waved at him: "No, not over here, it's the parking place for visitors. If you follow this road you'll come to the private parking." He kept talking in Tarnian so quickly that Eric couldn't follow. He suddenly fell very tired and in a lot of pain, as his wound was far from healed. He closed his eyes trying to fight against an acute fit of nausea but opened them again as he distinctly heard the phrase, "they aren't dead, thank Heaven!" He looked at Grant inquiringly.

The doctor wiped his brow. "Thank God," he whispered, then feeling Eric's stare turned to him and repeated in Westen: "The police agents, they aren't dead. Heavy injuries, both of them, but they will recover."

Eric nodded. Charlie switched to Westen and continued: "...but still, it's a darn bad business; the governor of the province was on the TV just now, and he's quite mad. Well, anyway, you are here and tomorrow is another day."

Dr. Grant who was now feeling much better about his own part in the affair noticed that his patient was close to collapse. "He should have stayed in bed at least one more day," he thought ruefully. Eric protested that he was fine, but in reality he needed the help of both of them to cross the square in front of a long two-storied building where they were to spend the night.

His room was quite comfortable, it had a bed, a table and two chairs and an adjacent bathroom, but Eric hardly cared for the way it looked. He was glad when he finally could reach his bed. Despite pain, he was so exhausted by all the events of the past several days that he soon fell asleep and slept soundly till the next morning.

Chapter 12. His Excellency Takes a Decision

The governor of the province was on the phone with the chief police commissioner. He was tired and couldn't help sounding irritated. "No, I can't allow your men to search the Abbey, Carmichael. His Excellency won't have it. Yes, I know we are a secular country and have a separation of church and state, that's the whole point, don't you see? The monastery falls under the authority of Church, not State.

"Yes, I understand that Uranians are pressing us hard, but what can I do? OK, I'll talk to him, but I don't think he'll change his mind, he didn't last time. Would his word be sufficient to you? Good, that's settled then." He hung up and stared in front of him for a couple of minutes. The Archbishop would soon leave for the Abbey himself, as tomorrow there was a national prayer day for all who worked in the agricultural sector, it being spring and all. He picked up his mobile again and dialed the number.

Meanwhile, Eric was blissfully unaware of all this. He had had a good night's sleep and was just finishing his breakfast and coffee. Dr. Grant, after checking on him, left as he was supposed to stay in the hotel for tourists.

"Also an alibi for him," stated Charlie, "plus the fewer strangers over here the better."

"Don't you have any work to do?" inquired Eric looking at his watch. "It's nearly 10 o'clock."

"Normally I do, but I'm on sick leave right now," confided Charlie. "I have already started working on your new documents. You are supposed to be a monk, aren't you? Prior Reginald going with the delegation himself, how d'you like to be his personal secretary? By the way, do you know anything at all about our liturgy and rites? You should at least look your part if you can't talk."

"Oh, I do speak Tarnian," answered Eric, "just not so fluent."

Charlie's dark eyes laughed. "You'll make old Reggie a good secretary. He usually does all the talking himself. Here, look what I brought you: a monk's habit. You'd better not try it on now, though, Dr. Grant says you are to stay in bed one more day."

Before Eric could answer, the door of his room opened and another monk appeared and said something unintelligible to Charlie. The latter suddenly looked very pale. He listened attentively, nodded and turning to Eric said: "His Excellency is here. He wants to talk to you. Personally."

Eric was stunned. "You mean the Archbishop, what was his name? Simanis or something? What the Hell…"

Charlie looked gloomy. "He apparently knows everything. The governor is livid about that chase of yesterday and wants to search the Abbey. Simanis says he's to talk to you first before he takes a decision. I'm afraid you have to go to him."

"What kind of man is he?" asked Eric, dressing hastily.

"Oh, he is fine, in his own way," answered Charlie slowly. "The point is, he doesn't seem to have much choice but…" Here he bit on his lip.

"You mean but turn me over to the authorities?" asked Eric tying his shoe laces.

"If you knew the kind of things going on over here," stated Charlie, "you'd understand he can't allow them to search the monastery. They aren't really after us, they are after you. Maybe, if you tell him what's it all about, he'll think of something. His Excellency doesn't like Uranians any more than anyone of us, that's for sure."

"You are not an Aarghean." This was a statement, not a question. Eric looked at the man in front of him. How old was he? 56-57? Probably somewhat older. Gray hair, gray-blue piercing eyes, he looked fit and too athletic for a man of his position.

Eric suddenly became aware of the fact that he hadn't shaved for a couple of days. Well, at least Charlie had provided him with a set of new clothes and got rid of the rags he'd been wearing, he thought.

"I come from Dakstra, Your Excellency, but I've spent the last five years on Aargh."

"Fought against Michael, didn't you?" asked the Archbishop curiously. Eric nodded.

"Now Mr. eh Wray, will you tell me what's it all about? Why do they want you dead so much?"

Eric thought a bit. It didn't really matter if he told the truth and Simanis would betray him, since the enemy knew it so far already. "I was a courier," he said, "and I was sent to Aargh to deliver a parcel and to receive another one in exchange. Uranians had been warned and thus I was arrested."

"Since you were arrested it means that the parcel was taken away from you, doesn't it?"

"Not exactly," said Eric. "It was actually a sort of a computer chip, and I disposed of it. So Uranians naturally wanted to know what I'd done with it. Later, when they finally understood it was out of their reach, they wanted to get rid of me so that I wouldn't disclose the information."

"What was it exactly?" inquired Simanis, not trying to conceal his interest any more.

"The plans of their new secret weapon, I believe," said Eric cautiously.

"And what have you done with them?"

"They aren't on this planet anymore and I'm the only one who knows where they are and can deliver them to Deltans, who are eager to get them, as you can well understand. So you see, Your Excellency, it's of vital importance that I leave this planet as soon as possible."

Simanis frowned. "Do Uranians know all this?"

Eric sighed. Should he tell the truth? Well, he didn't have anything to lose now.

"You see, Your Excellency, the man who had sent me to Tarna was planning to get rid of me. I have reasons to believe that he informed Uranians beforehand about my arrival and my mission, and that's the reason I was arrested after being there for three days. He sent another courier and that guy was supposed to receive the chip with the plans and to disappear as quietly as possible, while I was left to hang.

"However, things went wrong and those plans ended up with me. Before I was arrested, I sent a small parcel to the address that is known only to myself, outside this planet. Uranians were never quite sure they got the right man but after my escape they captured the other guy who had the misfortune to stay on Tarna to try and recover these plans and he talked before he died.

"I don't blame him," added Eric shuddering as he remembered his own treatment at the hands of the Uranians, but after the truth came out they really did their best to get me. I was in the rebel camp at that moment and heard the whole story from one of their chiefs, whose second-in-command, I'm nearly certain, was the one who betrayed us for the reward money."

The Archbishop was deep in thought for a moment and then asked: "Why did your superior want to get rid of you?"

"I told him that I quit. I've had enough of it all," said Eric.

"And what are you planning to do when you return to Aargh?"

Eric's eyes flashed. "I'll kill him!"

"Mr. Wray!"

"He had my best friend killed," said Eric defiantly.

"Under no circumstances can murder be right," stated Simanis.

"Why don't you tell it to him, Your Excellency?" retorted Eric angrily, but then realizing it was a pointless confrontation checked himself and continued more calmly: "OK, I'll talk to him first. He promised me a Deltan passport and a chance to start a new life. If he keeps his word, he'll get his plans."

There was silence and Eric understood that Simanis was trying to take a decision. Finally, the Archbishop spoke: "They told me they won't search the Abbey if I give them my word of honor that you aren't here. I have never broken my word in my whole life, Mr. Wray, and you must know by now I can't allow the search. I give you exactly three hours to leave the monastery. If you don't comply, I'll be obliged to deliver you to the authorities.

And tell that Stewart fellow that he could better go and visit his family for a couple of weeks, either. And that's my last word."

"Amen," whispered Eric.

Chapter 13. Another Escape

"So what now?" asked Eric somberly. "What am I supposed to do?"

Charlie looked unconcerned. "There is a tunnel starting in an old tower," he stated, "which is one Tarnian mile (1.8km) long and comes out in the mountains to the north of the Abbey. From there it's just a couple of miles to an excellent hiding place. We've used it more than once and Simanis knows it. Three hours is a generous time to pack. The only question is whether you are able to walk the distance, in your condition. But then, I'm going with you, too."

"Oh, I'll be fine," Eric assured him with the certainty in his voice he didn't really feel.

After hastily saying good-bye to Dr. Grant they left the novices' sleeping quarters, where they had spent the night, Charlie with a huge rucksack on his back. He refused to let Eric carry anything at all and was supported in his decision by Dr. Grant who looked very much displeased and muttered something about the inhumanity of dragging an injured man out of bed. He checked on Eric and declared that everything was in order but it was evident that he doubted if the latter were able to walk one mile, let alone ten.

"And you'll need medical assistance, too," he added.

"My friend who we are going to be staying with, is very good at treating ray gun wounds," said Charlie happily, "so that won't be any problem."

And thus they parted after shaking hands and Eric felt strangely sad saying farewell to someone who had been a friend yet again.

The tower where the tunnel began was more than a thousand years old and looked as if it could fall apart at any moment. Just as the building where Eric had stayed for the night, it was situated in the part of the monastery not open for tourists. The tunnel started in a cellar and after following the narrow steps which went steeply down, they found themselves in a long corridor with the floor made of stone slabs. Charlie switched his flashlight on.

"I hope this'll be enough for now," he said. "You'd better save your battery in case something goes wrong."

It didn't, though. They kept going down for some time, but then the tunnel made a sharp turn, and they had to start climbing. Eric tried to keep pace with his guide and bit on his lip more than once to fight the feeling of light-headedness. Finally, Charlie declared that they must be close to the end of it.

After another turn Eric saw dim light ahead and couldn't help breathing a sigh of relief. The tunnel ended in a cave where they spent the next hour and ate their lunch. A bar of chocolate and hot coffee out of the thermos flask partly restored his strength, but the longest and most difficult part of their journey still lay ahead of them.

Later, Eric thought that he would never have made it if not for Charlie who, though he looked rather thin in the normal hiking clothes he was wearing now proved uncommonly strong. The last kilometer or so he practically had to carry Eric together with a heavy rucksack of his own but his cheerfulness never left him for a moment.

They finally came to a lake in a narrow valley with dark green-blue water in it and pine trees all around. Eric wasn't insensitive to the beauties of nature, but hardly had an eye for them presently, though he got a general impression of peace and quiet. They went into the forest and there, several hundred meters further was a log cabin with slanted roof, painted red and white.

"There is no mobile connection over here, so it'll be a surprise for Frank," grinned Charlie. Eric, who was leaning heavily on his guide only nodded in exhaustion. The door of the cabin was open but they found no one inside.

"I'll look for him," suggested Charlie. Eric didn't answer, as at this moment he fell unconscious.

Chapter 14. Spirits in the Water

Frank Soester was of the same age as Eric and he was a big, robust guy with dark hair, a dark beard and brown eyes. He told Eric he was a geologist.

"You see," he explained, "this lake used to be a volcano crater once and there is still some activity going on, so we have to keep an eye on it. I'm going to stay here three more weeks and then someone else will take over."

"What if they search the house?" inquired Eric.

"Well, you haven't seen everything yet, have you?" chimed in Charlie. "We have a great hiding place over here, right under the floor. You won't be the first one staying there, either."

"You still keep talking too much," said Frank. "You can't stay with us anyway, because when they search the hut and find you, it'll be too suspicious."

"I wasn't counting on staying here," retorted Charlie. "I'd be bored out of my mind. Why do you think I'm carrying this?" and he pointed to his rucksack. "I'm camping in the mountains tonight and then I'm planning to stay with my aunt just as His Excellency suggested."

Though they couldn't use their phones they did have a radio and that's how Frank learned about the latest news. The first several days he insisted that Eric should spend as much time as possible in the cellar and only come out for a couple of hours in the early morning and in the evening, when it was getting dark.

The cellar was relatively spacious and well ventilated but it had no electricity or running water, only a small lamp working on rechargeable batteries and a chemical sanitary installation. Eric didn't really mind it since he spent most of his time lying in bed anyway. Frank had ample food supplies and since he was quite a good cook Eric soon discovered that he started putting on weight.

On the third day Frank woke him up early in the morning and informed him that according to the warning he had received on the radio, a search party was on the way so that Eric should try to keep as quiet as possible. They came half an hour later, searched the house and the small attic it had, asked all sorts of questions and left. Frank looked noticeably relieved.

"I don't think they will be coming back any more," he announced, "so that you are relatively safe now. Unless one of the village folks stumbles upon you and tips them off, which I doubt. They weren't really trying to do their best, either; just going through the motions."

"Does it mean I can get out of the cellar?" asked Eric.

"Tomorrow, or the day after, but you'll still have to sleep there, I'm afraid."

"Well, it's all right with me," said Eric, "but can I ask you what our next step is?"

"You'll stay here until your wound heals and until they stop searching, for a couple more weeks or so. By this time, we'll provide you with a new set of documents and send you to the capital where you'll get on board the ship and fly back to Aargh. That's all."

"Why are you doing all this for a perfect stranger?" inquired Eric. "You don't even know my real name. Why?"

Frank's face got hard for a moment. "It's not about you personally, Doug. It's a matter of principle."

"I see," said Eric.

Frank kept taking precautions for a couple more days, but gradually became more careless. By the end of the week, Eric felt well enough to go for a walk and sometimes they went fishing together. Frank was a silent type, the fact duly appreciated by his guest who didn't feel quite like talking himself. They shared the housework and cooking though Eric, not really accustomed to cook for himself, was quite bad at it.

After 10 days, he started feeling restless. He felt that it was time for him to move on. Frank wasn't that certain and thought they had to wait several more days, "until they completely stop looking for you," he said. Then the weather changed and they finally got some rain.

"Just what you need for fishing," remarked Frank, satisfied. That day he took Eric to another lake, higher in the mountains and also of a volcanic origin. It was smaller but deeper and according to Frank, there were some really weird fish living there.

"The locals believe there is a spell on it," he informed Eric. "And that it's a dwelling place of water nixes."

"You don't want to tell me you believe in local superstitions?" asked Eric.

His host merely shrugged his shoulders. "I've never met anything remotely magical over here," he complained, "though I keep hoping for a mermaid, preferably young and pretty."

The water in the lake was dark and the high pine trees all around it added to the atmosphere of mystery. Eric, who was rather superstitious by nature felt as if things were going to happen, and they did. Frank's hook got caught on something after the third attempt, and that something was quite heavy.

They pulled and pulled and then finally it came up – a dead body. It was a body of a man with dark hair which evidently had stayed under the water for no less than a week and it didn't look pretty at all. There were no documents or papers of any kind on him, just a wallet with some money.

"Well, what the…" swore Frank. "Now I'll have to warn the police."

"Wait," said Eric. "I have an idea. Look!" and he took something out of his pocket.

"What's this?" inquired Frank, surprised.

"My Tarnian passport," replied Eric. "I was supposed to destroy it, but by some strange reason I didn't. If I had been arrested, it wouldn't have helped anyway, and I had a feeling I might need it later on. Now it's my chance."

They put the document into the water for some time, to make it look like it had stayed on the dead body. Since the page with Eric's picture and all the information was laminated, it didn't really matter if the rest got damaged.

"There you are!" said Eric, stuffing the passport into one of the drowned man's pockets (he tried really hard not to look at the stranger's face while doing it). "Now that I'm officially dead, I'll probably finally be able to return back to Aargh!" ("And settle my account with Alec," he added silently).

Chapter 15. Return to Aargh

Their plan would never have succeeded if the authorities of the Free Republic had taken real trouble to investigate the matter. But they didn't. They were tired of the constant pressure from the Uranians and only too happy to announce that the case was closed. Douglas Wray was officially dead.

Three weeks later Eric found himself back on Aargh, in perfect health, a very lousy mood and with a passport of the autonomy on the name of Vincent Torr, 31, an investment consultant. In a new and expensive-looking business suit and with pockets full of cash he had little trouble to get access to the vault of one of the biggest Aarghean banks where his real passport, an Aarghean residence permit, his credit and debit cards and they keys of his car and his apartment were kept.

An hour later he was opening the door of his flat. It had been three long months but here nothing was changed. The apartment had been regularly cleaned by the room service and everything was in its place. He pulled out the top drawer of his writing table and took out a ray gun. It was about 3 p.m. standard time and he knew where he could find Alec Randall, all alone.

"It'll be a nice surprise for him," thought Eric. He changed into more casual clothes, suitable for the part of the city of Aargh he was going to visit. Looking too well off could only cause trouble in those quarters.

Two hours later he entered a dingy looking ugly office building in one of the long dreary streets of the shabbier part of the city. The street was practically deserted and he had no trouble parking his car. The old porter was quite satisfied after seeing his identity card, the one he had received from Alec long ago, signifying him as a freelance journalist working for an evening newspaper which had one of its offices in that building. Of course, nobody really cared that the office staff consisted of one person only present one day a week during certain hours.

5th store, room number 533 was the place where Alec Randall met some of his contacts on Friday afternoons. He usually stayed there alone till after 5 p.m., when the official working day of white collar employees was over.

The long dusty corridor was totally empty. The air was dry and hot, despite air-conditioning working on full capacity, probably because the equipment was out-of-date, just like everything in that building. Eric stopped for a moment before the heavy door with number 533 on it, then resolutely pushed it without knocking first.

 Just as he had expected, the door was open and when he stepped inside he saw Alec sitting in a chair behind the writing desk made of solid wood. A small ventilator on the left of him made a low zooming noise. There was a window on the right side of the desk with blinds put down which made the room darker. Alec turned away from the computer screen and stared at Eric in amazement for a couple of seconds but quickly regained his self-control. He seldom appeared surprised or moved by any sort of emotion. Alec Randall opened his mouth but didn't get a chance to say anything as at this moment Eric drew his ray gun.

"How does it feel to know that you are going to die, Alec?" he asked. Randall's face expression didn't change but his right hand made a slight movement.

"I wouldn't try this if I were you," Eric warned him. "At least, if you want to live an extra couple of minutes, that is."

The hand returned to its place. "Is this really necessary, old boy?" asked Alec with a slight drawl so characteristic of him. "Couldn't we just…discuss things?"

"What is there to discuss?" inquired Eric. "You used Irene to spy on me, you arranged Roger's death and you sent me to Tarna to die, tipping Uranians off about my arrival. You didn't expect me to come back, did you?"

"You are wrong about…well, nearly everything," said Randall casually. "I didn't use Irene. She fell in love with you on her own, not following my instructions. She doesn't work for me, either. We've just been good friends, that's all. As for Roger…Well, Roger was turning into an alcoholic rather quickly. He became dangerous for everyone involved. I'm sorry about your friend, Eric, but you have to admit that was the only way out. He'd been warned beforehand and he signed the papers. He knew the price he was going to pay but it didn't stop him.

"Considering yourself, I won't deny I used you as a decoy but I didn't tip the Uranians off though I wasn't surprised when you got arrested, either. Betrayal is the way of things on Tarna, as you have probably learned by now. I lost three couriers trying to get these plans before I sent you and…that other guy, may he rest in peace. I thought that at least one of you would make it, and I was right. Now will you take this thing away from my face? It makes me quite nervous."

"How do I know you are speaking the truth?" asked Eric.

"You don't," stated Randall calmly. "But had I really wanted to get rid of you, you would have been found in the same ditch as Roger, believe me. I don't need Uranians to do my dirty work for me. Will you now tell me what you have done with those documents? I need them badly."

Chapter 16. Back in the Game

Eric's hand holding the pistol didn't move. "How much are you prepared to pay for these documents?" he asked.

"So we are finally talking business, aren't we?" inquired Alec sarcastically. "We've made a deal, don't you recollect? You'll get your money when I get the papers."

"That's not enough," insisted Eric. "What about Deltan nationality you promised me? An opportunity to start a new life and all that sort of things?"

Randall shrugged his shoulders. "It's not for me to decide," he said. "But I can present the matter to the government."

"So you were lying yet again," stated Eric.

"I wasn't, as a matter of fact. I was talking about an existing possibility, that's all. Don't make it more difficult for yourself, Eric. You know you have no choice but to hand the documents over to me. If you shoot me now, you'll have the whole of our intelligence on Aargh after you."

"Are you so sure, Alec?" asked Eric quietly. "Nobody knows that I'm alive and back on Aargh. Nobody in this building has any idea who I am. Your body probably won't be discovered for a couple of days at least. What will you say to that?"

There was some quick trace of emotion in Randall's face, not fear but something very close to irritation. "Don't be a bloody idiot, Ericsson," he said tiredly. "You won't be able to get away with this, in any case not for long. Those who helped you on Tarna keep in touch with us. It's just a matter of time before it all comes out. I offered you a reasonable price, but we can discuss it further, if you wish."

"I want a Deltan passport," insisted Eric.

"I can't give it to you right now, but I'll tell you something else instead. Something that will probably interest you. How would you like to go back to Dakstra?"

The hand with the ray gun dropped down and Eric pulled a chair standing by the wall and seated himself.

"If that's another one of your jokes, Alec…" he began but Randall only smiled.

"I knew you'd be interested. While you were away, the amnesty was announced, on the occasion of the coming coronation of Michael. All political exiles are allowed to return. That includes you, of course. Coincidentally, I have some business to do with His Highness Prince Haakon, and it just came to my mind…"

"No," Eric interrupted him. "Never. Just arrange the Deltan residence permit for me and you can have the bloody papers for free."

"And what are you planning to do on Delta?" inquired Randall. "To work as an architect? You haven't ever graduated so you don't even have the necessary qualifications for a work permit. I offer you a diplomatic position at His Highness's court, as my representative."

Eric looked at him closely. "What you mean is that Delta isn't satisfied with the way Michael is carrying on lately and wants to encourage His Highness to try for the crown again. And you choose me to negotiate the terms. Am I right?"

"You have a lot of insight," remarked Alec Randall coolly. "I'd think that as a patriot, you…"

"There is no way, do you hear me, no way in Hell I'll fight on Haakon's side again!" said Eric vehemently.

"I'm not asking you to fight, just to talk. Why do you hate him so much anyway?" wondered Alec. "He did what anyone would have done in his place. It wasn't his fault you were stationed across the border. He saved the greatest part of his army when he signed the peace treaty offered by Michael. It was a small price to pay, you know. His Highness is ambitious and I believe he has a great potential."

Eric didn't answer; he was staring at the wall in front of him.

"And there is something else you'd be interested to know, too, I presume," continued Alec cheerfully. "Since Haakon is still officially a bachelor, his sister who has recently become a widow

56

returned home to stay with him and play the role of the lady of the house."

"What did you say?" asked Eric incredulously.

"I said that Lady Fraser whose husband General Fraser McAngus died three months ago is currently residing with her brother. As you have probably heard, their marriage was childless and since it's common knowledge that she could never really get accustomed to living in the North it's only logical that she would come back. Now you see that this mission will give you an opportunity to meet old friends. What do you say to this?"

"What exactly do you want me to do?" inquired Eric and Alec Randall smiled again. He'd won yet another game, and that knowledge was immensely satisfying.

Chapter 17. Did They All Die in Vain?

Eric was dreaming. In his dream he was back on Dakstra and it was a long, unbearably hot day in midsummer, the sort that makes one wonder if it would ever end. He was standing in a long line of prisoners with his hands tied behind his back. The news that Prince Haakon had finally signed the peace treaty reached his group too late and they had had no time to withdraw behind the river Sern and thus profit from the amnesty offered to all who had fought on the side of the rebels.

They had been surrounded early in the morning and lay down their weapons hoping for quarter but none was given. After they had been disarmed they were all lined up, with their hands tied, and the enemy officer would go along the line and choose every tenth man who was then dragged away and executed before their eyes. And on and on it went, and the sun seemed to stand still above their heads. The heat was intolerable. Would this day never end?

The officer, accompanied by a sergeant and two other soldiers was walking along the line again. This time he stopped right in front of Eric. Eric knew it was his turn now, but he didn't feel any fear. The only emotion which possessed him at that moment was burning hatred, hatred for the man who had called them to take up arms for the sake of the Fatherland and then betrayed them to save his own life.

"It's Lord Ravencroft's son," said the sergeant. The officer hesitated for a second, then turned his handsome arrogant face to the left of Eric and pointed his finger. "Take this one," he ordered. This one. Eric's childhood friend Andy Shultz. Andy, who had gone to university with him. Together with whom they chased after girls. Andy, whose mother was a widow.

As two of Michael's soldiers were taking him away to the place of execution he turned his head and there was such a look of horror and despair in his eyes that Eric thought he would never be able to forget.

"No!" he screamed, "No, not him! Take me instead! He's the only son!"

At that moment Eric woke up with drops of cold sweat on his brow and realized that he was quite alone in his own apartment on Aargh, in the middle of the night. It was in moments like this that he really missed Irene. He forced himself to get out of bed and went to the living-room where he took a whiskey bottle out of the bar. He poured himself a glass, sank into an armchair, drank it all at once and stared into the night.

It wasn't the first time he had had this dream, but it was first time he woke up screaming in that manner. In reality, he had never said anything. He wanted to, but he couldn't manage to produce as much as a sound. That day he had seen nothing but bloodshed and death since the early morning but he couldn't bring himself to watch Andy die. He closed his eyes at the very last moment, before the soldiers fired.

Andy died instead of him and was buried together with others in an unmarked grave, and he was brought to the capital in chains and had to undergo a show trial, and then there was a year in the prison camp, then amnesty on the condition that he would leave the planet so he became an exile. All that time Prince Haakon stayed in the safety of his own palace in Angharad. It had been five years since and now Michael was ready to pronounce himself king.

It all had started eight years ago, when King Richard disappeared without leaving a heir and Michael, who was the son of his younger sister was declared a regent by the parliament where he had a lot of supporters. He was called a regent but everybody knew he was after the crown. There was one problem though as the law strongly discouraged inheritance in female line.

Prince Haakon, the ruler of the three Southern provinces was the next candidate, but while Michael was the only nephew of the previous king, Haakon was but his second cousin (their grandfathers being brothers). He was then 27 years old and had ruled in Angharad for two years, since his parents' tragic death in a yachting accident.

Michael's own father had died a year before, officially as a result of some scientifically sounding disease but in reality, due to an overdose of a recreational drug and the evil tongues hinted that neither of those deaths was really accidental.

One thing was certain: Michael was insanely ambitious and he wanted to rule the country as a dictator, following nobody's wishes but his own. The ancient rights were daily infringed on, all opposition suppressed, independent newspapers persecuted and the law used as a hammer to come upon the head of anyone who dared to express disagreement. It was in this situation that His Highness Prince Haakon decided to try his chance and called all freedom-loving citizens to arms.

When Eric looked back later, he came to the conclusion that Haakon was probably expecting help from outside the planet as his small army was not a match for the federal forces which were at Michael's disposal. Dakstra was a member of the Baron Confederation, but the Barons declined to interfere letting the strongest win, and after more than a year of bitter fighting Haakon was forced to sign the peace treaty which further restricted the rights of the Three Provinces but was overall a much better deal than he could have expected, except for those unfortunate enough to stay on the federal territory after the treaty had been signed.

Those who were not shot on sight were hanged later, after short trials, sentenced to hard labor or driven into exile. Michael's power grew immensely but he still was only a regent, until recently, when the parliament took a special act which would allow him to put on the crown of Dakstra and in less than half a year he would finally get what he had always desired. Or would he?

Chapter 18. A Dream Turned Nightmare

Eric poured more whiskey into the glass, raised it up and drank to the memory of all those who had died trying to prevent this from ever happening. Now it looked as if their sacrifice had been in vain. He thought about his meeting with Alec Randall that afternoon.

Of course, he hadn't actually intended to kill Alec, unless it proved necessary for his own safety; not out of any moral considerations but simply because he was pragmatic enough to understand what the consequences would be, however that was exactly what he wanted Randall to believe and for a moment the latter did lose his cold indifference and showed that he was human after all.

However, he recovered rather quickly and managed to get the upper hand in the end, thought Eric somberly. He had heard the news of the coming coronation of Michael on Tarna, but he had no idea about Bell becoming a widow. And how could he know? He couldn't even remember when it was last time he had written home. Lady Ravencroft, his mother, usually sent several letters a year, but in her last letter, which he received before leaving for Tarna there was no mentioning of McAngus's death, probably because he was still alive then.

Eric wondered how he died, then thought of his widow, who before she became Lady Fraser used to be Princess Isabella, Haakon's sister, more than nine years his junior; and after her parents' untimely death spent summers with her widowed aunt whose estate bordered on that of Lord Ravencroft.

She was 16 then and he 18 and he could distinctly remember meeting her for the first time, with her flaxen hair, her light blue eyes and her white dress. His affection for her didn't go unnoticed, and Eric recollected how he and Raoul had once nearly cut each other's throats on the account of some words the latter had said on that topic.

Raoul was his eldest brother and there had always been bad blood between them, so that little provocation was needed on both sides to let the matter come to blows. They both were quite good with the sword, but Raoul, being three years older, taller and heavier finally drove him into the corner and then they were suddenly interrupted by their father.

Lord Ravencroft was really mad and after sending Raoul to stay with some distant family in the North asked Eric if he was fool enough to believe that the youngest son of an earl had any chance with a princess of royal blood.

"The girl is just playing games with you, Eric," he stated resolutely, "and like a romantic idiot you are, you fall for it."

Eric kept his mouth shut since he knew perfectly well there was no reasoning with his father when he was in such a mood, but he was convinced that Isabella really liked him and probably more than that, and when one is 19 years old it's easy to believe in the tremendous power of love.

And then that last summer came. He was in his 4th year at the university and he had just heard from Andy Shultz, who studied architecture together with him that the latter was planning to join the Rebel Army. Eric had been thinking about doing the same though he knew how much it would displease his father.

Lord Ravencroft was the leader of the Moderate party in the parliament of the Southern Provinces and had been against the rebellion from the very beginning, pointing out that, first, any civil war was a bloody and messy business; and, second, that their chances of winning against Michael were very slim.

Later Eric had to admit that his father had been right on both accounts but he was then 21 and asserting his independence. He had been renting an apartment in the capital, where he studied, which he shared with Andy, and after the examinations were over decided to spend a week with his family. His decision had been already taken though he didn't dare to announce it in person, knowing full well it would cause an enormous scene so he chose to write a letter later instead.

However, he confided in Isabella. He could still vividly remember that warm summer day, her aunt's tea house in the garden, the roses, the light breeze and Bell sitting next to him. He had very nearly told her that he loved her, but at that moment they were interrupted by her aunt, no doubt a well-meaning but quite irritating elderly person. That had been their last meeting but Eric was now sure that she shared his feelings and he was crazy enough to make plans…

He thought of her in the work camp and that made his life there more or less tolerable, until he heard of her upcoming marriage with Fraser. Was it but anyone else…General Fraser McAngus was more than twenty years her senior and had a horrible reputation. His first wife fell out of the window under strange circumstances and while some talked of suicide, others mentioned murder.

The worst part of the story was that the newspapers announced the happy couple had been engaged for nearly three years, right after his first wife's death, but were waiting for the mourning period to be over. For Eric, who realized only too well that Isabella was allowing his attentions while being officially engaged to another man, that was the last straw and after the amnesty was proclaimed he was only too glad to leave the planet, though if he had had any other choice he wouldn't have gone to Aargh.

It all happened long ago, and he tried to make the best out of things, there were other women in his life besides Irene, and frankly he never thought that he and Bell would ever meet again. However, that very moment that Randall mentioned her name and the fact that she became a widow, Eric knew he had to go back and meet her face to face. After all, he had a long account to settle, both with her and her brother.

Chapter 19. The Reception

Next Friday there was a reception in the house of Count Marchbold on the occasion of the engagement of his niece Louise, a pale young thing with red hair and spectacles, who had been his ward for the last year or so and Elza took a lot of trouble to get rid of her, no doubt, out of jealousy.

Louise was a daughter of the count's younger brother and some Deltan woman, who had been apparently never married to him, and when she turned 18 her parents sent her to Aargh in the hope that she would make a profitable match. Her aunt could never forgive her the fact that the girl was nearly 10 years younger and moreover, showed interest in Eric.

Elza didn't mind Irene so much; after all, she was just a common gold-digger and nearly of the same age, but her own niece was a different thing. Eric was perfectly well aware of all this but pretended that he wasn't. Luckily for everyone, soon afterwards he disappeared and the news of his death reached Aargh just in time to make Louise agree to accept a marriage offer from a young and promising Aarghean officer. That wasn't all the news Eric heard from Alec Randall as the latter had informed him that Irene was also going to get married.

"To a wealthy businessman, old enough to be her father and suffering from an incurable disease, as far as I heard," stated Alec. "He'll leave her a rich widow soon enough."

Eric only shrugged his shoulders. "You may send her my sincere congratulations and best wishes."

"Why don't you do it yourself?" inquired Randall. "I'm sure everybody will be delighted to meet you again, and your appearance will make all the local gossips shut up. And since I'll be there, too, we can settle this business with the documents to mutual satisfaction."

Thus Eric found himself in the residence of Marchbolds. Randall had provided him with an invitation, and he had no trouble getting inside. The count was talking to someone else when he arrived but Elza, who had just spent at least a quarter of an hour talking to one of her multiple best friends turned her head, saw Eric and gasped in disbelief.

She then grabbed his arm and demanded to know where he had been all that time and how he could leave his old friends all alone like this. Eric was rescued by the arrival of more guests, proceeded to congratulate the young couple and then escaped into a dark corner with a glass of wine though he thought by himself that hard liquor was the drink of choice while dealing with the countess.

He talked to a couple of acquaintances and assured them that he had been on a business trip to Tarna and stayed longer than planned due to an unfortunate car accident. He wasn't sure whether they had believed him and frankly, he didn't care, either. His thoughts were somewhere else entirely as he was leaving for Dakstra in the next two weeks.

It helped that he had officially stopped working for his uncle before going to Tarna. Stephen Ericsson was present as well. Eric nodded to him, but his uncle only turned his head away which was hardly surprising if one considered everything that had been said on both sides when they parted.

Irene appeared later on, accompanied by a sickly looking Aarghean in his late fifties. She didn't notice Eric at first, but then she looked around and saw him sitting there in the corner, all alone. He raised his glass to her and smiled, while she became deathly pale and leaned heavily on her fiancé's arm but soon regained her composure. She whispered something to him and they both disappeared into the crowd, but just as Eric was sipping his wine she suddenly stood right in front of him. Eric rose from his place and bowed stiffly but Irene apparently wasn't in the mood for polite formalities.

Her dark eyes flashed. "How could you?" she asked him indignantly. "How could you…disappear like this and make us all think you were dead?"

Eric laughed in spite of himself. "Darling", he said taking her hand and kissing it. "You haven't changed a bit. But remember, you are practically a married woman now. You found your happiness at last. Don't throw it all away because of…"

"I wasn't going to," stated Irene dryly, removing her hand. "I just wanted to tell you that it was a nasty trick to play, that's all."

"My disappearance or my resurrection from the dead?" wanted Eric to know.

"Both," said Irene and he laughed again. People started turning their heads and Eric became serious.

"You'd better not leave your fiancé alone, Irene," he said. "And fare thee well…"

For a moment, she looked as if she were going to make a scene, the suddenly changed her mind and asked him in a small voice: "Are you leaving?"

"Yes," said Eric calmly. "I'm going back home."

Chapter 20. The Moment of Truth

There is no telling where their conversation could have taken them from here were it not interrupted by the appearance of Alec Randall looking his society best. Eric was not sorry to leave Irene, in fact, he thanked his lucky stars that he finally got rid of her, but since the two of them had had a darn good time together, he thought that they could just as well part as friends instead of enemies.

And so they shook hands and he wished her a lot of happiness and prosperity in her marriage and followed Randall into the garden where they would not be disturbed. There he gave him a postcard depicting one of the famous Tarnian castles in 3-D form.

Alec whistled: "So that's where they have been all the time. Funny that nobody else thought of it."

"I sent this card the same day I got them," explained Eric. "And it pretty much saved my life. Had Uranians found those documents on my person when they arrested me I would have been shot the next morning. But they were never really sure about the role I played so they tried to use me to extract the information about Deltan agents operating on their soil.

"When they finally came to the conclusion that I couldn't be of much help with this, either, they promptly decided to get rid of me. I knew that St. Gottard was the place where most of the military executions were conducted so I had no illusions about my fate, and yet, here I am and I still wonder why."

"Yes, that's the problem with you, Eric," stated Randall, putting the card into his jacket's pocket. "You think too much. Leave all this metaphysics to the clergy, that's their task, to ponder God's will for men. Your task is much simpler. You will go back to Dakstra, meet your lord Haakon and do your best to persuade him that should he try again he'll get support from the King of Delta and from the Barons. Here, take this ring and put it on your finger. His Highness knows it and it will prove to him beyond the shadow of a doubt that you are speaking from my name."

"You know, Alec, you've never really told me what I am getting out of all of this," retorted Eric. "In case you've forgotten, I don't officially work for your government any more. By handing over these documents I fulfilled the conditions of our last agreement while you are yet to fulfill yours. I don't care for being ordered around by the likes of you."

Randall wanted to say something but Eric raised his hand. "There's one more thing you should know. You see, I'm rather keen on staying alive, so I took some measures to prevent any attempt on my life from your side. Should I die under suspicious circumstances, I'm sure your superiors will be delighted to know certain facts about your activities here on Aargh. And if you try to do it officially and make me stand any form of trial, I won't keep my mouth shut, either. That's all, really, and now we can go back to business. What is it I'm getting out of this affair?"

Alec swore through his teeth. "That damn Roger, he talked."

"Don't speak ill of the dead, Alec," Eric warned him. "Anyway, let bygones be bygones and let's discuss things instead."

To his great surprise, Randall laughed. "This time you get the upper hand, Ericsson. Don't worry, I can appreciate a worthy adversary, moreover, I need you. You'll get the money transferred to your bank account as soon as I check the papers you gave me and I'll make an official inquiry about your Deltan nationality. As for your mission on Dakstra, it's in your direct interests that you succeed."

"What exactly do you mean?" inquired Eric.

"Well, you always wanted to have the girl, didn't you?"

"She's a princess of royal blood," said Eric coldly. "I'm just a younger son of an earl."

"That's what you think," answered Randall. "But there's more to the story. Ask Lord Ravencroft about the circumstances of your birth, he can tell you more than I. And now we'd better go inside, before our absence becomes too suspicious."

"Stay where you are," snapped Eric. "What is it you are getting at?"

Alec Randall shrugged his shoulders. "Do you really want to hear it from me? That Lord Ravencroft is not your real father? And that were you not born on the wrong side of the blanket, you'd have a pretty good chance with whatever princess you chose? Are you now satisfied?"

Eric swore. "If that's another one of your lies…"

"It's well enough so, Ericsson," said Randall. "I can't waste any more time discussing your family troubles. And I suggest that you follow my example." He turned and went into the house, leaving Eric alone in the dark. His first impulse was to run after Alec and try to get the whole story out of him, but he changed his mind.

"In ten days I'll be on Dakstra," he said to himself. "And then…then I'll know for sure what I've always wanted to know."

Part 2.
THE QUEEN OF ELVES.

Chapter 1. Raven's Nest

It was nearly an hour by train from Angharad to Langton, a small village where Lord Ravencroft's estate was situated. Eric hadn't informed anyone about his coming. He decided that his arrival should be a surprise.

Dakstra, as nearly all the planets of the Galactical Sector X used the standard calendar based on that of Delta although its astronomical year was slightly longer, with the result that once in so many years an additional week was added to one of the summer months.

Right now it was spring there, so that Eric could still look forward to a couple of hours of light, when he stepped out of the train at 7p.m. Hardly anything had changed during these past five years. It was Tuesday and the station was practically empty. It was 45 minutes walking from there to his father's house and Eric spent them wondering how he would be met.

Raoul wouldn't be especially happy, that's for sure, but he dimly remembered that Lady Ravencroft had mentioned in one of her letters that he had been staying with his wife's family in the North, so it would be only her and Lord Ravencroft and the servants, of course. That would make everything so much easier.

Looking at his father's fields on both sides of the road, Eric wondered why he and Raoul could never really stand each other. As far back as he could remember they had usually been fighting whenever left alone for longer than five seconds. He had always attributed it to sibling rivalry but later started wondering if there was something else behind it.

The gates marking the entrance to Raven's Nest were meant more for decoration than for protection as the country around was generally safe. They were made from wrought iron and demonstrated a fine example of the workmanship of a very experienced local blacksmith living about a hundred years ago.

Eric looked through the openings between the metal bars at the stately house rising in front of him on top of a small hill and his heart started beating faster. It was nearly 8p.m. already and the gates were closed. If visitors were expected, they would stay open the whole evening; but this was obviously not the case so that he had to press the bell-button and wait for old Andrew Smith who was both Lord Ravencroft's personal driver and chief gardener to open the narrow side door for him.

As he had expected, Andrew appeared personally to inquire who would be so rude as to disturb the Earl's peace at this time of night. He was quite old-fashioned and kept rural hours. When he saw Eric his jaw dropped and he stayed there for some time looking incredibly silly.

"Andrew, be so kind as to open the door," said Eric finally. "I've been on my feet since the early morning."

The old man made a strange sound, waved with his right hand and proceeded to open the door.

"Mister Eric," he kept repeating, "you came back after all these years! I always knew you would! Right after they signed this amnesty bill into law!"

He embraced Eric, not trying to conceal his tears.

"Well, at least somebody in this household is glad to see me," thought Eric.

He came home just in time for the late dinner and the surprise of his parents couldn't have been greater. Lady Ravencroft hugged him and asked in her usual calm manner why he hadn't written. She recently turned fifty four and there were streaks of gray in her auburn hair but she still looked exactly as he had remembered her: a slender figure in a white dress (she had always liked white) with a kindly smile and a calm, self-assured manner.

Lord Ravencroft was five years her senior. Like every real Ravencroft he had raven-black hair while his piercing eyes were of a steely gray color, though he started turning gray as well.

Broad-shouldered and athletic, he had been a good swordfighter in his youth, and a cunning and scheming politician in his later years.

He had received his current high position of the Speaker of the House of Lords of the Assembly of the Three Provinces due entirely to his merits and he had never been afraid to express his opinion even if it was contrary to the desires of the Prince himself. Lord Ravencroft was the sort of man that even his enemies respected.

On the other hand, he was also arrogant, hard, intolerant to the opinions of others and demanded full obedience within his own household. His wife long ago accepted this fact and devoted herself to gardening, and Raoul knew better than to contradict his father to his face, but Eric had always been the black sheep of the family and treated as such.

On this particular occasion, however, Lord Ravencroft behaved quite decently, embraced his son, shook his hand and told him he was welcome back. During the whole of dinner he supported the small talk at the table, asked Eric questions about the state of affairs on Aargh, told him local news and didn't interfere at all when his wife suggested that now that her youngest son had finally returned it was time for him to find a nice girl and settle down at last.

Eric, who knew his father well enough, wasn't really deceived by this calm before the storm but contented himself with giving polite replies, smiling and eating, since Lady Ravencroft had always been known for keeping excellent cooks. That dinner was much better than anything he had ever tasted on Aargh and he told her so which made her blush and say quietly: "I'm glad you are back home, Eric."

However, when the dinner was over Lord Ravencroft stood up, looked at his youngest son significantly and said in not too friendly a voice: "There are a lot of things we still have to discuss, Eric. I'm waiting for you in my study in five minutes," after which he left the room. Eric, who wasn't in the mood to delay confrontation, kissed his mother's hand, told her he was really glad to see her again and followed him.

Chapter 2. Eric Learns Something New

Lord Ravencroft's study was a room with heavy vintage furniture, one half of which contained a good library including some collectors' items. The other half functioned as his home office where he spent the vast majority of his time at home.

Eric had rather nasty childhood recollections of having been brought to the room after he'd done something wrong for punishment and later, as he became older, being forced to listen to another of his father's lectures and he was determined to avoid Lord Ravencroft's sermonizing, at least, this time. He was nearly thirty after all, and had spent the last five, no, seven years of his life pretty much on his own, but the old habit of filial obedience was hard to break.

Lord Ravencroft didn't waste time on any subtle inquiries; he looked at his son and asked him directly: "Why did you come back?"

"Isn't it only natural, sir?" replied Eric. "I mean, I haven't been home for five years, and now that I've finally got a chance…"

"And in those five years we received exactly fifteen letters from you," interrupted his father. "Three letters a year was all you could spare for your family. Your mother cried her eyes out. Now that the amnesty has been proclaimed you've come back without as much as a word of warning and announce that it's because of your great love for your family. Don't be ridiculous. What's the real reason behind all this?"

Eric was silent and Lord Ravencroft continued: "You don't want to answer, do you now? Then I'll tell you. It's politics again, isn't it? Was the last time not enough?"

Eric raised his head: "This time it will be different."

"So I'm correct, after all," stated his father. "That ring on your finger. I recognize it. I have seen it before. You were sent here on a diplomatic mission, right? By Delta, I presume?"

"They offer us their assistance," said Eric. "They are worried about the way things are proceeding. Michael making advances towards Uranius, disregarding the treaties. Well, you know it all better than I do, sir."

Lord Ravencroft looked at him closely and shook his head. "You are a fool if you believe you can succeed against Michael. Unless Delta interferes directly, which they will never do. Do you realize that the only reason you are still alive is because I used all my influence to save you from the noose? Not for your own sake, but for the family honor and for your mother. But now I see that you've learned nothing. You are determined to end your life on the gallows. Well, let me tell you something: this time I won't interfere. I wash my hands in advance of anything which may happen to you. This time, Eric, you are entirely on your own."

"Whatever shall be shall be," said Eric stubbornly. "I'll accept my fate. But I'm inclined to think that you are wrong, sir. Michael is destroying our ancient freedoms, and it is the duty of every patriot…"

"Don't talk to me about patriotism," interfered Lord Ravencroft angrily. "Is it all because of her? Do you still have hots for this girl? Bloody idiot, she can never be yours. She's too much above you!"

Eric looked straight into his father's eyes and asked quietly: "Is she?"

There was a long pause and Lord Ravencroft was the first to lower his eyes. "How did you know?" he inquired. "Did Stephen tell you?"

"Yes, among other things," nodded Eric. "So it's true, then? You…you aren't my real father…"

Lord Ravencroft swore. "I probably should have told you long ago but the chance never seemed to appear. What exactly did he say?"

"That I was an ungrateful bastard and something along the lines of 'like father like son' and…other things, too, which I don't care to repeat."

"I'm sorry you had to hear it from him," stated Lord Ravencroft and wanted to add something else but Eric interrupted him.

"I am not sorry to know the truth. I insist on you telling me everything, sir. I have the right to know!"

"Your father was the Duke of Argentson."

Eric looked at his stepfather's face in disbelief. "The Duke of Argentson? That we learned about at school? The one who had been publicly beheaded on treason charges? That one? But that makes me…"

"The second cousin to both Michael and Haakon, yes," confirmed Lord Ravencroft. His stepson was speechless while his lordship leaned onto the back of his chair, closed his eyes and started narrating the story in a slow, monotonous voice.

"Your father and I went to school together and despite the difference in social position, we had always been good friends. He married young, as you probably know, and his wife who had been suffering from some disease died soon after the birth of their second daughter. The duke was left alone with two girls so everybody thought it quite natural when he hired a governess to teach them.

"This governess came from a good family and was young and pretty. The rest is history. In defense of your father I can only say that when he found out she was carrying his son he was planning to marry her, but soon afterwards he was arrested on the false accusations of treason. Before he was executed, he sent me a letter from prison, begging me to take care of the girl and his child and to keep his secret.

"My own wife at that moment was expecting, too, and it so happened that they gave birth within hours of each other. Unfortunately, Lady Ravencroft's labor was complicated and my son died before we could bring him to hospital. Your father was also dead by this time, so my wife suggested we adopt you and raise you as our own child. Nobody would know but the doctor and a couple of old servants who had assisted with labor and they were practically a part of the family. This would give you a chance of a decent upbringing and at the same time protect you from the king.

"We talked to your mother and she agreed. And that was that. Raoul never knew the truth though he undoubtedly has his own thoughts on the subject, and luckily, on the outside you look very much like me, probably because Ravencrofts are the distant relatives of the royal family of Dakstra, but those green eyes you inherited from your mother.

"Stephen found out later and it was one of the reasons I forced him to leave, but he had always had a grudge against you ever since. God knows I have always tried to treat you as my own son, but failed miserably. You are too much like your father, Eric."

"So it wasn't Lady Ravencroft..." said Eric pensively. "That's what Uncle Stephen was getting at."

"Well, one could expect that from Stephen," stated his stepfather coldly. "He has always been a pig."

"And my real mother, what happened to her?"

"She was a fragile young thing, pretty much shattered by your father's death and the fact that she had to part with her own child. One day she went for a walk and threw herself into the river. I'm awfully sorry!"

Chapter 3. An Ancient Curse

For a long time Eric didn't say anything, he was just staring in front of himself with unseeing eyes and Lord Ravencroft started getting worried when his stepson finally spoke: "My father's lands went back to the Crown, didn't they? His daughters didn't inherit?"

"No," replied the Earl. "The Duchy of Argentson can only be inherited through the male line. Since your father was the last of his family and died without an heir, it returned to the king and officially became the protectorate of the Crown. There has been no new Duke since your father's death."

Eric tried hard to conceal his emotion but his eyes flashed in spite of all his efforts: "That's the greatest news I have heard since …well, since forever. This gives me a chance to…" He didn't finish his sentence.

Lord Ravencroft sighed: "I'm sorry, Eric, but you are illegitimate. You have no legal claim to the lands and the title. None whatsoever!"

"I don't…for now," agreed Eric, "but all will change when we win the war. Then I can claim them not by the rights of blood, but by the rights of conquest."

"And how many men must die to satisfy your ambition?" asked Lord Ravencroft dryly. "Or is it of no consequence to you?"

"You are mistaken, sir, if you think that only my ambition drives me forward," answered Eric indignantly, "but then, we never could see face to face on this issue. I would have tried anyway, now I have another reason to do so. My father's line must not die out. It's my duty to my family to try and restore it, don't you understand? The fact that I'm illegitimate doesn't change anything as there were precedents when such as I did inherit. I'm sure His Highness will agree. By the way, does he know all this?"

"Possibly," admitted his stepfather reluctantly. "The prince knows a lot more than some people give him credit for, but he keeps his knowledge to himself. Eric, that idea of yours is sheer madness. It will cost you your life and it will cost the South a lot in blood and treasure, and the result will be total and utter subjugation to the North, without even a shadow of former independence. Delta is not to be trusted. That's their way of doing things, stirring trouble here and there, but never committing themselves. Delta will never support the losing side. When the things get tough, they'll abandon you to your fate."

"I have reasons to believe they won't, this time," stated Eric. "As for our independence, we are losing it every day and soon there will be none left. Don't you realize, sir, that the situation is dire? You are the speaker of the Assembly and the governor of Angharad (the capital of the South and its main province bore the same name), as such you wield a lot of influence. Your help would be invaluable."

"I'm also currently the Head of the Security Council, the position, which as you know, rotates," Lord Ravencroft informed him. "And I'm telling you, 'No'. You may persuade Haakon but you'll never get the necessary support either of the parliament or of the council, let alone the Church. Theodosius will never approve another war."

Eric suddenly smiled. "I've thought of him. His Excellency won't object when he realizes he'll get a chance to become His Eminence, of this I'm sure. With him on our side we'll win both the Council and the Assembly."

By this time his stepfather was starting to lose his temper which usually happened when he had a conversation with Eric for longer than ten minutes.

"When I hear you talk like this, I start regretting that they didn't shoot you back in '99," he declared angrily.

"It may yet happen," replied Eric calmly, "but as long as I live I'll never stop trying. And that's my last word."

Lord Ravencroft looked at his stepson in surprise. Emotional outbursts used to be more typical for him than the grim determination which now sounded in his voice. Suddenly all his anger disappeared.

"That's your father's blood speaking in you, Eric. He had been exactly the same and look where it brought him. They say there is an ancient curse lying on any man of the Drakenvuur blood; he'll never be satisfied with what he already has and will always try to reach for the stars. Your father was like that, Prince Haakon is like that and you are like that. I tried to stop your father when he openly confronted the king but he wouldn't listen and neither will you. And yet, I saw it as my duty to try."

"Well, sir, then you have done your duty," said Eric rising up. For the first time in his encounters with his stepfather it was him who showed that the conversation was over.

"I'm sorry we are on different sides but I'm afraid it can't be helped. I won't stay here long so as not to bother you. Tomorrow I'm leaving for the capital. And now, if you'll excuse me, I'm very tired after my journey and have a lot to think about."

And with these words he turned and left.

Chapter 4. Isabella

The next morning about 10 a.m. Eric was driving along the narrow streets of the center of Angharad in his vintage red two-seater which he had received from his father after finishing school. It was a beautiful sunny day in the end of April and he had the window open and the radio on.

Lord Ravencroft, despite all his objections, had provided his stepson with a pass giving him direct access to the Prince which was more than Eric had hoped for and this circumstance appeared to him a lucky one.

He reached the palace at 10.15, parked his car in a designated place and had little trouble at the gates. A young guard checked his papers, then asked him if he were Lord Ravencroft's youngest son and what his business was. Eric replied that he had just returned from exile and wished to see His Highness on a private matter.

He added something vague about future career prospects as it appeared wise to him to conceal the real reason of his visit. South was full of Michael's agents and the palace was probably not an exception.

The guard nodded, phoned someone and let Eric in, adding that his colleague would bring the latter to the reception room. Eric had been to the palace once, long ago, with his stepfather and he faintly recognized the square with the statue of Haakon's great-great-grandfather, the fountain and the lawn, the main stairs and the long narrow passages. He was brought to the first floor, ushered into an empty room and told to wait there.

"His Highness will be informed shortly," said the guard and left Eric alone with his thoughts. The room had a window which offered a fine view of the palace garden, several rather uncomfortable chairs, a low coffee table standing on a rug in the center of the room with several magazines lying on it and two doors: one through which Eric had come inside, the other leading to the inner quarters.

Eric was prepared to wait for quite a time so he first scanned a couple of magazines and then stood up and looked out of the window. He could see a tea house in front of him and some rose beds. The sound of the door opening made him turn abruptly but to his surprise instead of Haakon he saw a woman with blond hair dressed all in black. As their eyes met she uttered a strange sound, as if she were choking and rose her hand to her throat.

For a moment Eric became deathly pale, but since he had been more or less expecting to see her, his self-control returned sooner than hers. He bowed stiffly and said in an official voice: "Your Highness."

Isabella (for it was her) suddenly blushed which made her look much younger. "Eric…Is that really you? You came back, after all these years…" Then she checked herself and added in a steadier voice: "What a pleasant surprise! Welcome home! My brother will be delighted to see you again. We were all wondering what had happened to you, you know…"

"Did you really?" inquired Eric ironically, but she didn't notice.

"Do sit down and tell me everything about yourself."

"As Your Highness wishes."

This time Isabella couldn't ignore his manner any more.

"Why this official tone, Eric? There was time when you used to call me Bell."

"This time was long ago, Princess," Eric informed her. "Before you got married to Fraser McAngus. By the way, allow me to express my sincere sympathy on the occasion of his untimely demise." The sarcasm in his voice was unmistakable and Isabella looked hurt.

"I don't have the right to the title any more, you know. If you insist on being formal, then call me Lady Fraser. I hope you won't mind if I keep calling you Eric though, it reminds me of the good old days."

Eric shrugged his shoulders. "Were they really good? But whatever pleases you, my dear, I mean, my lady. Anyway, you asked me what I have been doing. I spent all these years on Aargh, working as an architect and only recently returned to Dakstra. I hope that His Highness can offer me a job as a member of his security staff or something along these lines. And what about you?"

Isabella didn't answer, she was staring at the ring he had on his little finger. Eric hastily turned the stone inwards but it was too late.

"Security staff…" said Isabella slowly. "That's not why you came back, is it?"

"Darn," thought Eric, "how much does she really know? She never used to be interested in politics before."

"One guess is as good as another, Princess," he said aloud. "I have a business to discuss with Haakon, but that concerns him and him alone."

"Politics again," said Isabella bitterly. "No, don't bother to deny it, I see it in your eyes. That's why you came back. And I thought…"

"What exactly did you think?" asked Eric coldly. "That I came back because of you?"

"We used to be friends," whispered Isabella. "Now you talk as if you hate me."

"You are entirely mistaken, Lady Fraser," said Eric rising up. "I still have perfectly friendly feelings for you. And as your friend I may recommend you to keep yourself occupied with feminine things such as interior decorating or gardening and leave politics to men."

That made her very angry, but before she could think of an appropriate answer the door opened again and Prince Haakon entered the room.

Chapter 5. An Interview with His Highness

His Highness was about to turn 35. Tall, broad-shouldered and athletically built, with black hair typical for men of his family, piercing blue eyes and high cheekbones, he was a remarkably handsome man. His popularity with women was legendary and news and gossips about Haakon's love life had dominated the society columns since he was sixteen. Eric by now had spent exactly one day on Dakstra and couldn't avoid hearing about His Highness's new romantic interest.

Haakon was also a charismatic leader of men, a skilled politician and overall, an insanely ambitious individual though with years he had learned to conceal it. He could by turns be either arrogant or friendly and a lot of people were deceived by his simplicity of address and his disregard for the usual formalities which served as a good cover for his iron will and his drive for dominance.

Eric had last seen him about seven years ago in the Memorial Square in Angharad where he was addressing the volunteers departing for the front lines of which Eric was one. At that moment, he had been ready to die for the Prince and the Fatherland.

Haakon hadn't changed much since then though he looked slightly older now and the lines around the mouth became harder, but he still produced an impression of someone full of energy, vitality and hidden power.

"I'm glad you are back, Eric," said Haakon and it sounded as if he really meant it. Eric, who hated His Highness with a passion made an effort to control his countenance, bowed his head and said "My lord" in a steady voice.

The prince looked at his sister significantly and Isabella left without saying a word. He sat down and with a gesture invited Eric to do the same.

"I'm quite busy this morning but when I heard that the youngest son of Lord Ravencroft desired to see me I thought I could spare a couple of minutes. What is it that you want to talk to me about?"

Eric looked right into Haakon's eyes and turning the ring upward showed it to him. "Your Highness will undoubtedly recognize this."

The prince stared at it with some surprise, and then laughed suddenly. "So that's why you came back after all. I should have known. What message do you bring?"

"That Delta offers Your Highness their full support, financial and otherwise should you choose to make another attempt for the Crown of Dakstra."

Haakon's face stayed motionless but his eyes flashed: "Financial and military, you mean? On what conditions? And where do you figure into all of this?"

"I'm authorized to speak on behalf of the King of Delta," replied Eric. "If you accept this offer you'll get a war loan, logistical support, military advisors and through the influence which Delta exercises over the Barons, the possibility of recruiting volunteers for your army on several planets. And the Barons' consent for the military operation, of course. In exchange, Delta desires the rights to the exploitation of all the mines in the Rastar area, a permanent military base, exclusive trade agreements and the written statement in the constitution of Dakstra that any alliances with foreign powers should be approved by Delta first."

Haakon stood up. "In other words, they want us to become their protectorate. They will dictate our trade and foreign policy and undoubtedly, interfere into the domestic affairs to a certain degree as well, when they see fit. And you, what is it you want?'"

Eric, too, rose from his chair. He was nearly as tall as the prince. "My father's lands and title."

"Your father's...?"

"I mean my real father, the Duke of Argentson."

His Highness looked at him closely. "How did you find out? Did Lord Ravencroft tell you?"

"His brother did."

Haakon sighed. "Eric, you are a bastard, I mean, illegitimate. I know it's not your fault, but it's against the law and tradition."

"My father's lands went back to the Crown," said Eric stubbornly. "The new King of Dakstra will have the right to dispose of them as he chooses, which includes rewarding those who served him well."

"Is that all?" inquired the prince. "Or is there anything else?"

"That. And your sister's hand in marriage."

His Highness was silent for a moment, contemplating what he had just heard. He stood with his back to Eric so that the latter couldn't see his face, then turned abruptly. "I accept. Now let's sit down and you'll tell me everything I should know."

Chapter 6. There Is a Price on Everything

Eric had a very long conversation with the prince, during which they exchanged information, made their plans and discussed their strategy. Haakon wielded a lot of power in the Southern provinces, but he couldn't take such a decision alone. The Assembly had to vote on the issue and it was doubtful whether they would go against the recommendation of the Security Council, whose Head Lord Ravencroft had been quite explicit in rejecting the idea.

Then there was Archbishop Theodosius, who had a semi-permanent place on the Council. Officially, he was there in the capacity of a spiritual advisor, representing the interests of the Church. Unofficially, he had a habit of interfering everywhere and often swayed the opinion of the Council to one side or the other.

Scheming and ambitious, he was very popular with common folks, who viewed him as some sort of a saint, probably for the same reason His Highness was popular, too: Theodosius lived a simple life, had a friendly address and spent a lot on charity. He had also a gift of eloquence and his sermons were widely attended.

Unfortunately for Eric, he had a long-standing feud with Lord Ravencroft and the two couldn't stand each other. Eric despised the Archbishop whom he considered the finest example of the hypocrisy of the clergy and he was pretty sure that the feelings were reciprocal.

In Theodosius's eyes he was a son of a heretic and dangerous at that since Lord Ravencroft was one of the greatest supporters of secularization and restricting the power of the Church. He had long thought how to solve this problem, but luckily for him, the Archbishop had one weakness: just as his earthly lord, he was very ambitious.

"You just have to hint that once you are king, you'll make him a cardinal, Your Highness," he stated. "In my opinion, that'll be enough. If Theodosius consents, the Council will agree, and then the Assembly. It's that simple."

Haakon hesitated. "Are you really prepared to openly challenge Lord Ravencroft? After all, in the eyes of the world, he is still your father."

Eric shrugged his shoulders. "He knows where I stand. The price we are going to pay is high, but I'm convinced that Deltans will be better masters than Uranians. He thinks otherwise. It's just a matter of taste."

Haakon was of the same opinion though he refrained from announcing it. Instead he pointed out the necessity of keeping this information strictly secret until the parliament takes its decision.

"I can't give you any prominent position right now, Eric; after a five years' absence it'll be too suspicious, but I'll grant your request to join the security staff if you agree to swear an oath of allegiance to me."

"I've already done it once," reminded Eric, "when I joined the rebellion."

"It's not the same," explained the prince. "You must swear personal allegiance to me as your liege."

Eric went down upon his right knee, raised his right hand and repeated the words of the ancient oath swearing to stay loyal to the person he hated even more than Alec Randall. So that was the price he personally had to pay. Despite formally belonging to the Reform Church of Dakstra and in private declaring himself an agnostic, Eric superstitiously clinged to the faith of his ancestors who had worshipped Allfather and considered oath-breaking the crime worthy of the worst torments of Hell.

"I accept your service," said Haakon simply. "And I think I don't have to remind you that the punishment for breaking this oath is death. And now the ceremonial part is over, let's talk about more practical things."

Eric spent the rest of the day wandering around the palace, learning his new duties which appeared few in number since he was expected to become something like a personal aide to the prince and making acquaintance with some of his new colleagues.

He would officially join the prince's service tomorrow so it was his last day of freedom. He didn't see Bell even once but learned that though, since Haakon was a bachelor, she managed his household; His Highness spent virtually all of his time with a certain Laura or Lady Laurentia whom he had brought home after one of his visits to Dakstra's capital, that this Laura, who used to be an exotic dancer before she met the prince, was extremely beautiful and that the two women hated each other.

Through the years, His Highness had had a lot of mistresses but his affairs usually were of a short duration and he never let his women forget their place, but everybody agreed that the way he carried on with Laura, treating her more like his wife than his mistress, was downright scandalous and highly insulting to Her Highness. He's totally lost his head this time, was the general conclusion.

Eric was intrigued; he was curious what sort of a woman she was to exercise such an influence over the prince. His wish to meet her was granted that very same evening when his sovereign informed him that since the next day Eric would start working in his new capacity, one of his duties would be to accompany his lord to a private party in the house of a certain lady where the Archbishop would be present, too. They would discuss their business there.

Chapter 7. Brother and Sister

It was six o'clock in the morning when Eric woke up the next day. He had been provided with a small apartment in the palace which consisted of a bedroom, a sitting room with a small kitchenette in the corner and a bathroom. His apartment was in the same part of the building as Haakon's private quarters.

The sun was shining brightly and when he looked out of the window he saw a rose garden. Tempted by the view, Eric quickly got dressed, went down the stairs and entered the garden through a small side door. He was nearing a teahouse when he became aware of someone else's presence and the next moment, recognized Isabella.

In a simple white morning dress, she was cutting roses with heavy garden scissors and her delicate hands looked ridiculously big in the protective gloves. She turned her head when she heard Eric approaching and looked at him closely.

"Good morning," said the latter and stopped abruptly, unable to proceed. Fresh morning air brought color on Isabella's cheek making her uncommonly lovely. For a moment, Eric forgot how angry he had been with her and just stared at the young woman in front of him as if he saw her for the first time in his life, but then checked himself.

"Your Highness," he added stiffly.

"Good morning," answered Isabella with a smile. "Your habits haven't changed much, I see! You have always been an early bird. I heard you got the job, didn't you?"

Eric nodded. "Today is my first official working day," he informed her and added without any particular reason: "And I'm to accompany your brother to a private dinner."

Isabella colored slightly. "So you are going to meet her, I presume."

"You mean Lady Laurentia?" inquired Eric innocently.

"I mean this Northern harlot my brother dragged home," replied the princess angrily.

"His Excellency Theodosius is expected as well," proceeded Eric. "I wonder the "Holy Father" approves of such parties if the things are as you describe."

"Why do you dislike him so much?" asked Isabella, surprised.

"I'll answer your question if you tell me why you dislike Laura so much," responded Eric.

"Because my brother has turned the royal palace into a brothel," she declared. "It's bad enough he is totally under her thumb, but all the men surrounding Haakon sooner or later fall under her spell as well."

"I heard Lady Laurentia is extremely beautiful," stated Eric. "As for the Archbishop, well, isn't he supposed to be an example of meekness and disdain for all things worldly?"

"You are just as bad as him," retorted Isabella. "You are planning to persuade my brother to begin a new war using Theodosius as a tool. It's hardly for you to judge. What did Haakon promise you in return?"

Eric shrugged his shoulders. "What one usually does in his situation."

The princess bit on her lip and said, after a pause: "You know Eric, I was always attracted to you because…because you were so different from those around me. While they were pragmatic and cynical, you were romantic and idealistic. You were motivated by other things than just by power and status. But now you've changed. You are exactly like everybody else. My brother, His Excellency, all the others. It breaks my heart."

"Really?" asked Eric losing his self-control for a moment. And whose fault is this?"

"Are you trying to say it's mine?" inquired Isabella speaking with a visible effort.

"Can you deny that you were flirting with me while being engaged to another man? Had it been anyone else, it would have been easier to bear, but Fraser…"

"I was not flirting," protested Isabella. "I have always seen you as a friend. Surely, you understood there could be nothing serious between us? As for Fraser, my brother insisted upon this marriage. I had little choice in the matter."

"Surely you must have noticed it was more than mere friendship on my side?" asked her Eric angrily. "So why did you encourage me? No woman can be so blind or so stupid as not to know when a man is in love with her!"

For a second, the princess looked as if she were going to burst into tears but then collected herself. "Must I really explain this to you?" she inquired, then turned abruptly and ran away.

Isabella was rather surprised to find her brother waiting in her living-room. She muttered the usual words of the ceremonial greeting and curtsied more out of habit than genuine regard. Haakon nodded, accepting her obeisance.

"I wanted to talk to you," he stated watching his sister arrange the roses in a vase. "What do you think of Eric?"

"That he is dangerous. And that he hates you, but you probably know it yourself."

The prince shrugged his shoulders. "His personal feelings don't interest me in the slightest. Do you think he can be trusted?"

"I think he'll drag you into another war which can very well cost you your country and your life. But you don't seem to mind."

"If I'm not mistaken, there was a time when he was…well, showing interest in you. He probably still does. He's always been a romantic type."

"I wouldn't describe Eric Ericsson as romantic," retorted Isabella. "Cynical and bitter are the words I'd use."

"A man can be bitter and still very much in love. An intelligent woman will be able to use it to her advantage."

Isabella seated herself next to her brother and inquired: "Do you expect me to spy on him? If so, the answer is definitely 'no'."

"May I remind you that I'm not only your brother but also your lord and sovereign?" asked Haakon.

"You can't force me to go against my conscience," said Isabella haughtily. "Not again. Find another tool for your purposes. I won't betray Eric for the second time. Is it clear?"

"Perfectly," Haakon assured her. "A very good morning to you, sis."

Chapter 8. The Meeting of Conspirators

Laura lived in the business center of Angharad, on the third floor of a new apartment complex. The fact that she had her own house was Haakon's tribute to the rules of decorum but it hardly deceived anyone, especially since he spent most of his free time with her.

Other guests besides Eric and the bishop would be Lord Vernone, Haakon's chief-of-staff and General Raileigh, his interior minister. Those two were the prince's most important allies and if he could persuade them to support the cause of independence, it would be a great step towards the South's freedom.

Both Vernone and Raileigh who had arrived earlier and were waiting for the prince outside the apartment building were rather surprised to see Eric follow them inside, while two other guards stayed by the car, but they refrained from commenting. They both knew by now that His Highness always had reasons for whatever he did.

Haakon, undoubtedly, was in the possession of the key, but he kept up appearances to the last; ringing the doorbell. Laura was apparently waiting for them as the door opened almost immediately.

Eric who was by now standing next to His Highness stared at the woman in front of him: the gossips of the palace hadn't lied – she was extremely beautiful. Lady Laurentia's hair was red and her eyes were of the color of the sea on a sunny day. She was tall and slender and looked not older than twenty six.

Dressed in a low-cut evening gown in the color of her eyes, she stood there smiling and Eric was stunned. And yet he didn't lose his common sense and it whispered to him that the woman who could captivate such a man as the prince for such a long time possessed much more than just a good figure and a pretty face. She was an adventuress, exactly like himself. He could understand why Bell called her a witch as there was something enchanting about her.

It all flashed through his mind while they were being introduced to each other. Laura looked at Eric with some interest and welcomed him. She had a pleasant voice and all her movements were uncommonly gracious and yet, there was something predatory about her.

The archbishop was still not there and while they were waiting, Laura served the drinks and sat down at the piano. Vernone and Raileigh talked to each other in low voice, glancing at Eric significantly, His Highness seemed to be totally absorbed in his own thoughts, and Eric was watching Lady Laurentia play.

She started singing an old ballad about a young knight going about his lord's business who meets the Queen of Elves riding in the woods and rejects her advances since he has a fiancée at home. He ends up with a dagger in his heart.

"Beware of the Elven Queen," sang Laura and at that moment she slightly turned her head and their eyes met. For a second, it seemed to Eric that he was that knight desperately trying to find his way through the woods and that the Queen of Elves was before him, offering her friendship. He slightly shook his head, trying to get rid of the vision. Laura laughed and started singing a comic song.

His Excellency was nearly 45 minutes late and could hardly conceal his displeasure at the sight of Eric. He held his tongue though and restricted himself to frowning every time he looked in Eric's direction.

They ate and drank and Laura did her best to play the role of the hostess, but when the dinner was over, instead of removing herself as it was the custom to let the men discuss their business, she stayed right there and listened attentively to what her lord had to say. Haakon briefly explained the situation and turned to Eric who suddenly felt unable to speak.

"Gentlemen, it's now or never," he said finally. "Michael is going to be crowned in a couple of months and will rule as a dictator, not a king. He's getting stronger by the day and we are getting weaker. It's the question of survival, that's all."

Vernone and Raileigh started talking at once, demanding to know what guarantees they would obtain from Delta and whether they could afford the war. Eric patiently answered all their questions.

Theodosius was silent, until Haakon asked for his opinion, and then said soberly: "The Church can't approve the bloodshed which will be the inevitable result of the secession. The Scriptures teach us to honor those placed above us, which includes Michael, who with all his drawbacks, is still a loyal son of the One Church, which is more than I can say about some others."

Suddenly Laura spoke: "Is he?" she inquired in her melodious voice. "Then why does he tolerate that horrible Lord Hammerstone who by all accounts, has sold his soul to the Devil?"

They all turned to her. "Surely, you don't believe these wild stories?" started Lord Vernone, then checked himself.

Laura shrugged her shoulders. "Michael is jealous of any rivals, including the princes of the Church, that's all.

"Our religion certainly allows self-defense, doesn't it?" inquired Eric. "If we proclaim independence and Michael attacks, it will be a war of aggression on his part and the defensive war on ours. If our Heavenly Father deems it fit to grant us victory and the true son of the Church becomes king, he will need a spiritual counselor to give advice and to represent Dakstra among other Confederation planets."

Theodosius stared at Eric for quite some time as if trying to read his thoughts, then turned to Haakon. "Young Ericsson is right," stated the latter, "Dakstra needs a new cardinal, young and energetic, the one who will undertake his mission with zeal and vigor. Unfortunately, His Eminence Reginus is too old and infirm to defend the rights of the Church which, like everything else, are trampled upon in the North."

That settled the question. The bishop rose from his place and said solemnly: "In this case, Your Highness, you have the Church's blessing."

Haakon rose, too, and they all followed suit. The prince's eyes flashed: "Let's drink to our victory!" he exclaimed and they all did and threw their glasses into the fire.

"And now," continued His Highness, looking around: "We must decide what we are going to do next."

Chapter 9. Eric Addresses the High Lords

The very next morning Eric was on duty in the Royal Hall. It was huge and empty, used only on ceremonial occasions, with the princely throne of Angharad in the center and crown jewels kept under lock and key in a gigantic safe, the real reason why it had to be guarded day and night.

He used the time to prepare the speech for the extraordinary gathering of the parliament which was to be held in three days. The Hall had two doors, one opened into a gallery and that was the one he had to guard, the other one, on the opposite end led into a corridor which would take you to the private quarters of the prince.

While Eric was contemplating what exactly he would say to the High Lords of the Upper Chamber, it opened suddenly. Startled by the sound, he raised his eyes and saw Isabella.

"And what do you think of her?" she asked approaching him. Eric was amused.

"Do you mean Laura? I think she is the Queen of Elves."

"The Queen of what?" Isabella looked puzzled.

"Well, haven't you heard that story growing up? About the Elven Queen riding on her horse on stormy nights luring the lonely travellers away from hearth and home? That's Laura. Where did your brother find her?"

"Somewhere up North. I don't know. Is it important?" inquired Isabella. Eric shrugged his shoulders.

"I was just wondering. Anyway, Bell, you'll be probably glad to hear that His Excellency gave us his blessing." The princess bit on her lip.

"What is it you want, Eric?"

His green eyes narrowed a bit. "I want to get back what is mine, that's all."

"I don't understand you."

"It's probably for the best."

"Well, keep your secret then," said the princess, trying hard to feign indifference. "Just answer one more question, will you? Is it true that the Upper Chamber will meet in three days to discuss your proposals?"

"You are very well informed," said Eric, bowing slightly.

"There are still those in this palace who honor my father's memory," remarked Isabella. "I must go now. See you later," and with these words she left.

"Is she jealous of Laura?" wondered Eric. "Or did she use her as a decoy because she wanted to know more about our plans? Probably both. Is it important? No, they won't be able to stop us, not with Theodosius on our side."

And yet, he wasn't so sure of himself when, three days later, dressed in his best suit he was standing in front of the Upper Chamber of the Assembly of the Free Men of the Southern Provinces preparing to address them.

In fact, he had a sinking feeling in his stomach. All these men were older than himself and occupied a higher position in society and one of them was his own stepfather, Lord Ravencroft, and he looked downright hostile.

His Highness and the bishop were present, too, but Eric was convinced that His Excellency would never support the losing side, and as for Haakon, after a short speech he had pushed Eric forward obviously preferring to stay in the background this time.

Eric was on his own and he knew it. He looked around desperately. Faces, faces everywhere. Not one smiling, not one remotely friendly. Tense, alert, some nearly threatening like that of his father. His stepfather, really, but old habits are difficult to break and Lord Ravencroft was the only father he had known.

At that moment, a side door opened and a slender figure wrapped in a dark cloak quietly slipped inside. The hood covering the head and face fell back for a moment, but it was enough for him to catch a glimpse of red hair and discern fine features. Laura! The only woman to ever have been present at the Assembly meeting. The only woman who would dare to do it.

She stood behind a pillar and looked at him and smiled. That smile gave him the self-assurance he needed so badly. When Eric finally addressed the audience, his voice was firm and he spoke with an air of authority about him.

"My lords, the hour is upon us. The future of the Fatherland, of our way of life, of our whole civilization is in your hands. The decision you are going to take today will probably be the single most important decision in your life…"

When he finally finished speaking he was out of breath and not one person in the hall, not even his stepfather, stayed unmoved. Haakon rose up from his seat of honor in front and joined him, and so did Theodosius, to his eternal surprise.

"My lords," said the prince. "You have all heard what young Ericsson had to say. I will now ask you to consider it carefully before you cast your vote. Thank you."

The bishop said nothing. He just stood there beside them, and it was enough.

Lord Ravencroft took over. He did a thorough job presenting the arguments of his own party, though the presentation was somewhat lacking in emotion. Eric had expected more opposition from him.

They were asked to decide whether the Chamber agreed with secession or not. Eric's heart pounded in his ears. His hands were clammy. The results of the vote were exhibited on a huge screen above his head. Before he could turn and look he heard his stepfather's voice announcing that their proposal got nearly 60% of the vote. They won!

He looked into the corner where Laura was hiding, a triumphant smile upon his face, just in time to see her disappear through the side door. One last glance before she vanished into the darkness, and she was gone. Yet Eric felt that since that moment on there was something tying them together, an invisible thread which could only be severed by the death of one them.

He couldn't just stand there daydreaming though, there were still lots of things to discuss and decisions to make and so he forgot all about Laura for the time being.

Chapter 10. A Lunch Invitation

The next three weeks were a whirlwind of activity. At the end of this period, things had progressed so far that though officially secession wasn't announced yet and the Lower Chamber still had to vote for it, it was basically decided upon by everyone of any importance.

Lord Ravencroft tacitly admitted defeat and returned to his castle entirely in line with his "I wash my hands" attitude and Isabella finally succeeded in talking to Eric for at least ten minutes straight without making any catty remarks. Not that her cattiness had produced any impression on him, he just continued to tease her which initially made her mad, but after some time they both fell into a more friendly mode of conversation.

In fact, Eric had to admit to himself that it almost felt like the good old days again; when they used to be friends. That was the thing about Isabella which initially had attracted him, she wasn't like all the other girls, there was a sense of companionship about her. She was certainly not as empty-headed and vain as Irene though it was probably unfair to compare the two. It was easy to treat Bell like a pal.

One sunny day in the end of May she invited him to lunch with her and he agreed. They went to an old café in the historical center of Angharad which was very popular among the University students. Eric used to visit it quite often together with Andy. Now it seemed to have been ages ago.

Isabella looked very proper in her dark two-piece with a long skirt as she was still officially in mourning, and she put on large sun glasses as well but nobody appeared to recognize her anyway. She noticed the shadow passing over his face and thought by herself that they probably shouldn't have come over here, and yet there was something she wanted to talk to him about and by some reason it was easier to do it there than in the palace.

"Eric, do you by any chance know what happened to Andy? I mean Andy Shultz. He was reported missing in action. His mother contacted me after I came back. She is such a nice lady and…"

Isabella didn't finish her sentence shocked by the reaction of her companion. Eric became deathly pale and swallowed hard.

"Are you not feeling well?" she inquired, but he only shook his head.

"I'm fine," he said, still talking with difficulty. "It's just…I have been thinking of him as well. We used to come here together. So you've seen his mother? How is she doing?"

"As well as one can expect in her circumstances," answered Isabella. "She thinks he must be dead, but this uncertainty is gnawing at her. She thought I might be of help but I could find no official information about his fate. You were in the same company with him, weren't you? I thought you might know…"

"He is dead all right," stated Eric gloomily. "I saw him die."

"You must go and talk to her," declared Isabella. "It will give her great solace to know that his friends were with him in his last minutes."

"Are you sure?" asked Eric. "Do you know the manner in which he died?"

This time it was Isabella who turned pale. "Wasn't he killed in action or something? Answer me, Eric!"

"He was executed right before my eyes. By the Northern firing squad. He was buried in an unmarked grave with all the other guys killed that day. Are you sure his mother should know?"

The princess looked horrified. "I thought the terms of surrender were that quarter was to be given to anyone who laid down his weapons," she said in a small voice.

"Not to those who were stationed across the border, it wasn't," Eric informed her.

"I'm sorry," she whispered, unable to look him in the eyes. "It must have been a terrible experience, but at least…at least you are still alive."

"A sergeant recognized me. He must have been a Southerner," said Eric. "So they took Andy instead of me."

She touched his shoulder. "You shouldn't blame yourself, Eric. That's not your fault. That was just fate."

"It's not myself that I blame," retorted Eric coldly. "Not any more. But getting back to the point, if you insist I can go to Andy's mother and tell her all this, but personally I believe it's better for her to keep thinking he was missing in action."

"Truth is always better than pretty lies," replied Isabella. "We will go there together, you and I. Tomorrow morning, if you have time."

"I do," said Eric, "but only a couple of hours, because as you probably have heard the day after tomorrow we are leaving on a diplomatic mission to Jokusfelt."

Isabella's face expression changed instantly from one of a deep contemplation to that of alertness. "And is it true that Lady Laurentia is going with you?" she inquired.

Eric nodded. Isabella drank the rest of her wine in one sip and her eyes flashed: "That's unbelievable. My brother can't do it. Not even he can go so far! After all, he is going to negotiate his marriage to a princess of the Royal House of Jokusfelt and he is dragging his mistress along! Apparently, he can't bear to be separated from her for even one week!"

"You can better discuss this matter with him," replied Eric shrugging his shoulders. "I'm not the one who decides such things. His Excellency is going with us, too, and he doesn't seem to object so it must be fine."

"She will be the only woman among the delegation," pondered Isabella. "What will be her official position?"

"Haven't they told you?" inquired Eric, amused. "There will be some household staff travelling with us. Laura will be disguised as one of the cleaning ladies."

Isabella laughed suddenly. "She is as proud as the Prince of Darkness himself. I wonder how she will like her new role."

"That remains to be seen," remarked Eric and asked for the bill.

Chapter 11. A Stunning Discovery

Jokusfelt was a planet of ice and fire, famous for its volcanoes and geysers, which lay at a 2-days' journey distance from Dakstra. It was strategically important because its king occupied a senior position in the Council of the Baron Confederation and the Royal Family of Jokusfelt was one of the most ancient in Galactical Sector X. The story went around that their ancestors were Northern fairies, which strictly speaking was nonsense, and yet a lot of people believed it.

King Harald had had a son and three daughters, and the girls' beauty formed a subject of many discussions, but several years ago his eldest daughter disappeared under strange circumstances. The official narrative was that the princess got lost during a hunting party in the forest and probably met with a horrible accident, however, the evil tongues hinted that her disappearance was voluntary and that there was a man behind it all, or even worse, that she left home to live a life of an adventuress somewhere in foreign parts. One thing was certain, King Harald never mentioned her name and neither did his courtiers.

The king was in his early sixties, so his red hair had streaks of gray in it, and his look was proud. The bride-to-be was his third daughter (his second one had recently married the chairman of the Confederation Council); she was not present during the negotiations, as it was a custom among the Barons that women were totally excluded from any political affairs, and they were discussing, among other things, the military help which the Lord of Jokusfelt could extend to his prospective son-in-law.

Harald's son Olaf was sitting at the right hand of his father and he did most of the talking. The king himself was not a man of many words, but when he spoke everybody listened and even Haakon was impressed. Yet, they seemed to be going nowhere and after three days of the negotiations, Eric was bored out of his mind.

Jokusfelt had a cold climate and it was the middle of the winter there, too. The thermometer showed 20 degrees below zero, everything was covered with snow, all the women outside wore long thick coats completely covering their figures and they hardly had a chance to meet any ladies inside the palace. Wherever Laura was, she kept herself out of public eyes, too. They were given a whole wing of the Royal Palace and the cleaning staff had their own quarters. In any case, the lady who came to clean his room every day was an old hag both in appearance and in behavior.

Every evening they had a meeting all together and Theodosius droned on about the most insignificant matters, which was getting on Eric's nerves. "Well, it's only for a week," he kept saying to himself.

He saw Freya, the princess in question, only once and then from a distance, when she was allowed by her father to make acquaintance with the prince. Accompanied by her mother, she spent exactly five minutes talking to him, then disappeared in the long narrow passage. She was a pale, elegant thing with long flaxen hair and light-blue eyes, and Eric had to admit that she possessed a sort of haunting beauty for those who were into that sort of thing. He himself preferred women with more vivacity and character.

On the third day, the negotiations ended early and he had some time free of duty. Elevated to the rank of a lieutenant of the Guards on the account of the diplomatic mission, he functioned more or less as Haakon's personal secretary and was attached to his Highness's person for nearly 24 hours a day, but now the prince wanted to talk privately to Olaf and so it happened that Eric was allowed to do as he pleased and he decided to investigate the palace.

It was awfully old and Eric, as an architect, had a professional interest in the way it had been built. He appreciated the Northern style in architecture with its simple elegance and found that the later Gothic elements only added to its charm.

There was an art gallery on the second floor which had plenty of family portraits and other paintings, some of them more than a thousand years old. Eric who drew himself was fascinated by the collection and went from one picture to another forgetting all about the time. The collection was rather disorderly, with no attention given to the proper sequence and thus he encountered a modern painting among some old ones.

It was the portrait of the royal family taken about ten years before, with King Harald, his wife and all their children. Eric looked at the eldest princess with perhaps more than a common interest. She had red hair and the eyes of the strange greenish color and a bold face expression so untypical for someone of her age and social position. She reminded him of someone. Where had he seen this face before?

"Not, it can't be true," Eric said to himself. "The whole idea is preposterous." He waved his hand in front of his eyes, then looked again. The face in the picture kept smiling at him. Laura's face, only ten years younger.

When he finally came back to his room to change for dinner, he encountered the cleaning lady. In her dark long uniform dress, with a white apron and cap, she was busy dusting the desk.

"Good afternoon, Miss Holster," said Eric politely, hoping that she would take the hint and disappear. The lady turned and laughed.

"Laura!" exclaimed Eric, stunned. "What are you doing here?"

"Tss," she answered, putting a finger to her lips. "Not so loud. Nobody is supposed to know I'm here."

"What, were you not sent by His Highness?"

She shook her head. "I need to talk to you, Eric. There is something you must know. But I can't tell you now. There is too little time, as they will miss you at the dinner table. Can I come tonight?"

Eric nodded. Even ugly clothes couldn't conceal how beautiful she was and her proximity made his heart beat faster. Eric tried his best to conceal his feelings and feign indifference but he wasn't sure he actually succeeded.

"Till tonight then," said Laura and left the room.

During the whole long dinner party while Prince Olaf was discussing technical details of the upcoming trade agreement between the two planets and His Excellency Theodosius was preaching a sermon about one's duty to sacrifice everything on the altar of patriotism, Eric kept thinking about Laura.

There could be little doubt of the real reason she wanted to visit him alone in the dead of night, but did she act out of her own free will or according to Haakon's orders? Eric wasn't eighteen anymore and had trouble believing that his charms alone would make her disregard the very real consequences were their affair to be discovered. If His Highness sent her, there could be but one reason for this, but did it really matter? He had desired her since the first moment he'd seen her and tonight she would become his.

Laura came as the clock was striking twelve, this time wrapped in a dark long cloak, the same she had worn during the Assembly meeting. She had only a see-through lacy nightgown underneath.

"I wanted to warn you," she started, but Eric pulled her to himself and saying: "We'll talk about it later, these nights are awfully short, at 6 a.m. His Highness will expect me," proceeded to remove her cloak and everything beneath it. She didn't resist in any way and they spent the next hour in mutually pleasant activities and he was convinced that she had enjoyed it just as much as he himself.

"Why did you come?" he asked her later, sitting in bed and looking at her body, strangely white in the moonlight. "Did Haakon send you?"

"Oh no, of course not. He'll kill me if he finds out. In fact, he'll kill us both."

"I'm not afraid of him," Eric informed her. "Now are you going to tell me it was love at first sight? It'll certainly boost my self-esteem."

"I do like you," admitted Laura. She sat up, too, and pulling a sheet wrapped it around her shoulders. "There is something about you, Eric, something which makes me think we are similar in many ways."

"We both lost our birthright," said Eric looking at her attentively but he could trace no sign of emotion in her face. Her self-control was admirable, or was he simply mistaken in his assumptions?

"Haakon doesn't trust you," she continued, "and that's what I wanted to talk to you about. And the circumstances were such that I lost my head. We all have our moments of weakness, you know."

"His Highness is wise not to trust anyone," agreed Eric. "If I were him I wouldn't trust Theodosius, either. He's a snake as ever has been, so Haakon should ensure he'll commit himself so far to our cause that he won't betray us half way to the scaffold."

"He thinks you want the crown for yourself," stated Laura significantly.

"Who, Theodosius? Then he is more stupid than I thought."

"I meant His Highness."

"Really?" inquired Eric. "What makes him think so?"

"You may be illegitimate, but the blood in your veins is the same as his and you are just as ambitious, Eric. You could go far and you are younger."

"I swore an oath of allegiance to His Highness," replied Eric. "I don't intend to break it. And, anyway, Haakon is popular with common folks, but nobody cares about me. The whole idea is ridiculous. Why, the Church would never agree. I'm not even of the proper religion."

"People changed their religion for less," said Laura quietly. "And the bishop doesn't really care who will give him the cardinal's hat, you or Haakon."

"Well, maybe he doesn't care, but I do. It's bad enough I have to listen to his speeches from time to time, but I sincerely can't imagine myself having to deal with him on the regular basis. I do dream of a crown, but rest assured it's only a Duke's crown. Now you may go and tell His Highness I'm perfectly loyal to him in thought and deed, so he doesn't need to assassinate me as a precaution or whatever he was planning to do."

"I'm sure he won't go so far," said Laura rising up. "But you are mistaken, Eric, if you think he ordered me to come here, so if you wish to live happily ever after, you'll do good to keep our encounter secret. So long," and with these words she put on her clothes and left the room.

Chapter 12. Playing With Fire

The negotiations lasted longer than they had expected, but Haakon finally managed to achieve the majority of his objectives. He would receive a war loan to be paid back by Delta's money, volunteers for his army, weapons to fight the war and Harald's support in the Confederation Council.

As for his engagement to beautiful Freya, it remained conditional on the success of his enterprise. The girl was only sixteen anyway, so she could wait. His Highness was more than satisfied, and as the summer progressed so did their plans.

In the end of June the first volunteers had arrived, the money transfer was complete, Southern factories were working overtime producing weapons and ammo, Eric had just returned from Aargh where he had had an important meeting with Alec Randall and the Lower Chamber of the Assembly voted for the secession. Their dream had become a reality and the rebel flag was proudly displayed above the palace tower.

Michael, who had to delay his upcoming coronation because of the way things were developing, reacted by sending an ultimatum which was rejected. His next move was to send the troops and there was an outbreak of fighting in the border province of Delawar. For some time it was uncertain which way the war would go but the Barons, no doubt, pressed by Delta, after holding an emergency meeting on the matters of security unanimously declared that they would not tolerate any attempt to eradicate the independence of the Three Provinces.

Under the very real threat of their sending an expeditionary force to "restore peace and order", Michael had nothing left to do but to sign another treaty granting the South its independence and restoring all the ancient rights. It put both adversaries into a difficult position. The planet was now de facto if not de jure divided into two parts, and neither of them was satisfied.

Haakon realized only too well that he lacked the strength to win over Michael's army, which was in no small way supported by the Uranians; but he also realized that the Barons wouldn't approve of such a move, either. After all, they had voted for a two-state solution.

Michael retained the wealthier Northern part of the planet, but he couldn't be crowned king any more, which was his chief ambition. His Uranian handlers weren't satisfied, but refused to interfere openly in order not to disturb the fragile balance of power in Sector X and provoke Delta into an open action. Both sides had to look for another solution of the crown succession issue, but for now, things had settled down a bit.

Eric had been working overtime functioning more or less as Haakon's liaison officer. He'd been to the front several times, took an active part in the siege of Rhoon, the capital of Delawar where he got a slight concussion, had to spend a week in hospital and then left for undercover negotiations with the representatives of the Barons and Delta on Jokusfelt with King Harald acting as a mediator. It had been a risky trip since Michael's space ships were hunting them but they managed to escape.

By the end of the war, Eric acquired the rank of lieutenant-colonel and the position of the chief of the security staff. He was also totally exhausted. He never really fully recovered after the month he'd spent in Uranian dungeons and after the Yule's festivities were over and he resumed his work, he collapsed right after an important meeting they had held in the Upper Chamber.

"It's just fatigue," the doctor told him when he finally came by. "You need to take it easy, Colonel, for a couple of days."

Haakon, who was also present, nodded in agreement. "Why don't you take a week's leave, Eric, and go visit your family or something?"

"Sure," replied Eric. The whole week of vacation was more than he had had altogether in half a year.

It was about 3 a.m. when he finally reached his bed. His breakdown was hardly surprising considering his constant lack of sleep, but the doctor gave him some sleeping pills and so he floated away and only woke up because someone was shaking him by the shoulder. To his surprise, it was Isabella.

It was some time since Eric had seen the princess let alone have a talk with her and he suddenly realized that he had missed her. All that time he was carrying on with Laura though their meetings were few and never lasted long. The war was over, the date of Haakon's wedding was chosen, and it was probably the realization of this which really drove her into Eric's arms, though with Laura one never really knew. One thing was certain, she wasn't planning to stay in Angharad once His Highness was married.

"It's 10 o'clock in the morning," said Isabella reproachfully.

"Well, I never," he said smiling. "Have you come to play the part of an angel of mercy?"

The princess nodded. "I've brought you a cup of coffee. And this room looks like a pig sty. In fact, your whole apartment does."

Eric sat up and stretched himself. "I've no time for such things," he announced.

Outside the sun was shining brightly and it was a beautiful winter day. He had better living quarters now, with a big bedroom, a spacious living room, a real kitchen and a bathroom and though cleaning service appeared twice a week, he had to admit, looking around, that it was rather messy.

"It needs a woman's touch," he grinned drinking his coffee. "Maybe if you stay for a couple of days, you can clean it up."

"Why don't you ask Laura instead?" retorted Isabella. "Your affection for her is hardly a secret to anyone."

"Why, Bell, I do believe you are jealous!"

"No, I'm not," she stated angrily. "The fact that I was asked to take care of you for a couple of days doesn't mean I'm planning on functioning as your maid!"

"Have you been asked to take care of me? Who did it?"

"My brother. You scared everyone to death yesterday by your fainting fit."

"They'll miss me like a headache," shrugged Eric his shoulders. "Bell, since you are here, how about breakfast? Doctor told me I must stay in bed for a couple of days."

She did make breakfast, started the dishwasher and went as far as to wash his clothes as well. "The rest you will have to do yourself," she announced. "I'll come again to check on you in the evening."

"And my lunch, then?"

"I'll send someone!"

She left and Eric stared at the door for some time. How much did she really know about him and Laura? One thing he was certain about, he wasn't really in love with Laura. She fascinated and thrilled him, but love was something else entirely, or was it?

That evening he was reading in bed when Isabella came along. She had a puzzled look on her face.

"I've had a talk with Haakon," she said significantly. "Is it true he promised you the Duchy of Argentson if you win the war?"

"What else did he tell you?" inquired Eric putting his book aside.

"That you have a lawful claim to it!"

"It's true because the late Duke was my father!"

Isabella looked at him incredulously. "S-surely you can't be serious..?" she stammered, but without much conviction in her voice.

"I'm perfectly serious," Eric assured her.

"But that means…"

"That we are family, sweetheart. One big happy family. Aren't you thrilled by the idea?"

"That explains a lot of things," pondered Isabella. "But you do realize by now you can't win the war, don't you?"

"Not by a direct attack, no, but there are other ways."

"A coup?" wondered Isabella. "An assassination attempt?"

112

"You really don't expect me to give an answer to this, do you now?"

"Eric, you'd better stop before it's too late!"

"I can't," he said. "None of us can. Dakstra can have but one lord. It's either your brother or Michael."

"Or yourself, maybe? Or doesn't your ambition go that far?"

He grabbed her by her hand and pulled her to himself. They both were breathing heavily by now.

"Whose side would you choose then, Princess?"

"Let me go," she protested. "You are hurting me!"

"And how do you think I felt when I heard about your marriage? Answer my question, Bell!"

She shook her head indignantly. "Surely you understand what Haakon will do to you if he hears of this? You are playing with fire!"

"That's what I like to do, play with fire! Have been doing it all my life."

She was sitting on the bed close to him now and he heard her heart pounding. It wasn't an opportunity to lose and he took his chance. Initially she answered his kiss, but then gathering her last strength pushed him aside and slapped him hard across his face.

"Well, thank you very much," he said rubbing his cheek. Suddenly she burst into tears and ran away.

Part 3.

THE CURSE OF THE DRAKEVUURS.

Chapter 1. A New Intrigue

"So, gentlemen," said His Highness Prince Haakon looking at the men before him. There were five of them: Lord Vernone, his chief-of-staff, General Raileigh, his interior minister, Lord Sutherland, his new prime minister, Derek White, the secretary of the Right Reverend Father Theodosius and an officer of his secret police and Eric Ericsson, a colonel of the Security Service.

White and Ericsson had worked together before and were more or less friends as they were close in age to each other. The three other men were in their late forties and fifties. They weren't particularly enthusiastic about the new plan, but what else could they do? The situation was such that an urgent decision had to be made.

It was an early spring day in March of the year '07, according to the standard calendar used in the Galactical Sector X and Michael, the ruler of the Northern Provinces of Dakstra, was getting married in a month's time, to a Uranian princess. Though the civil war and the semi-official partition of the country which had followed, prevented him from proclaiming himself king, this marriage would strengthen his position and his claims to the throne, especially if there was a heir produced shortly afterwards.

Haakon, on the other hand, could only marry Princess Freya if he became the king of the whole Dakstra, an event which he was just as far from at the moment as the year before. They had to act quickly and if that meant taking risks, so be it.

"So, gentlemen," he repeated. "Now that you've all heard the plan, do you have any suggestions? Anything to add?"

"My lord," said White. "His Excellency the Bishop doesn't trust me. He also insists that his nephew goes with us, instead of Colonel Ericsson, who is highly unsuitable in his eyes due to being a heretic, that is to say, not belonging to One True Church."

"That's absolutely out of the question," answered the Prince resolutely. "I need both you and Ericsson in Troon."

"Would it not be better if we informed His Excellency of our plans?" insisted White. "In that case, he'd probably be more cooperative."

"No," retorted Haakon. "Theodosius will never agree to be used as a decoy. He must know nothing about this whole affair. You both go."

"But Your Highness, Colonel Ericsson had been pronounced persona non grata…"

"That was long ago," Eric interrupted him. "We now have peace with the North."

"Eric, you are on their blacklist. I don't think it's really wise for you to go there."

"The same is true about you, Derek," answered the latter with a smile.

"I don't have such a horrible reputation," objected White. "Everybody knows your role in that whole secession business. It's too dangerous."

"They won't dare to do anything to me. I'll be a part of the official delegation and the one responsible for security as well. It's a diplomatic mission, for Pete's sake!"

Derek White didn't look convinced. "They can try to assassinate or kidnap you."

"They can do the same to Theodosius's nephew."

"He doesn't know anything of importance, and you do! I just don't get it why both of us have to go."

"Because, as you have pointed out yourself, I have a reputation. The coup leaders won't talk to you. Our contact in Troon informed us that they would only negotiate with a person close to His Highness. Since none of gentlemen present here can leave his post, I'm the only one available."

"I still don't understand why we can't take Lieutenant Wiggles as well, just to humor His Excellency," said White, exasperated.

"Because we won't have time to babysit him!"

"Gentlemen, enough already," interfered Haakon. "Major White, the colonel is right. He'll have to go to Troon personally, whether His Excellency likes it or not. He'll have to accept the situation and make the best out of it. My lord Vernone, did you want to say something?"

"Can we really trust the other side?" inquired Vernone. "It may very well be a trap. General, it was one of your men who had arranged that meeting, wasn't it? What can you say?"

"You've read the report yourself, your Lordship," replied Raileigh shrugging his shoulders. "I've chosen my best man for the job, and I think we can trust him as far as anyone can be trusted in these difficult times. Michael isn't really popular in the army these days, you know. His officers may be Northerners, but they can still be patriotic and disdain the union with Uranius, our ancient enemy."

Lord Vernone bowed stiffly and turned to Sutherland, who was his second cousin on his mother's side. "And what do you think of it, Roger?"

"I don't particularly like the idea of a coup," answered Lord Sutherland indifferently, "but I guess all is fair in love and war."

He was about ten years younger than both Raileigh and Vernone, and being of a different generation, shared His Highness's opinion that the end justifies the means. Haakon thought it was a good moment to end the meeting.

***

"And so you are going to witness Michael's wedding, aren't you? Laura ran her thin musical fingers through Eric's black hair. "It's a rare honor, you'll be one of the few select Southerners present."

"I don't see it as such," replied Eric lazily. "I'm going there as a security officer, that's all."

"Oh, really?" laughed Laura. "Am I to believe that our worthy Theodosius will face danger while taking part in a wedding ceremony? Someone else would suffice."

"He is the Bishop of the Southern Provinces. He can't have some junior officer in charge of his security," explained Eric. "So I have to go."

"Come on, you and His Excellency can hardly stand each other and everybody knows that he wanted his nephew to go instead of you."

"Is Wiggles really his nephew? Or, perhaps, a closer relative?" inquired Eric pulling Laura's hair. He was half lying on the coach in her living-room with a big cushion under his head and she was sitting next to him wearing something black, lacy and see-through, with her red hair hanging loose around her.

"Don't be nasty," said Laura. "Of course, he is. Why, the boy isn't much older than twenty which means that the Bishop was about 45 years old at the time of his birth and must have outgrown this type of sentiments, if he ever had them to begin with."

"Oh, I believe he did," stated Eric, "and probably, still does. Take the way he looks at you, for instance."

"Don't change the subject," interjected Laura, her hand left his hair alone and travelled to Eric's bare chest. "I'm not interested in the romantic entanglements of Theodosius. I've never heard that he keeps mistresses anyway. I just want to know why they chose you to go as his security guard."

"His Highness wanted it," answered Eric. "I really can't tell you more than that. In fact, I'm not supposed to discuss it with anyone."

"Not even with me?" She bent over him with her lips nearly touching his.

"Not even with you, my dearest Laura," responded Eric but not very resolutely. "And anyway, I have to go soon."

"You've only been here for an hour or even less."

"Well, we used our time wisely, didn't we? It's nearly midnight."

Laura suddenly jumped off the couch and stamped her foot. "Don't lie to me, Eric Ericsson! You are going there because you are meeting someone. Someone important. Someone who promised Haakon to get Michael out of his way."

Eric sat up and started collecting his discarded clothes from the floor and putting them on.

"If you already know everything so well, why ask me?" he said calmly, buttoning up his shirt.

"Because I don't want you to go."

"Strange, Derek White didn't want me to go, either."

"He was right," agreed Laura. "I believe it's a trap and Haakon is sending you because he wants to get rid of you."

"Why would he want such a thing?" inquired Eric, putting on his sweater.

"Because he is afraid of you. You are getting too popular. Then there is Isabella who is in love with you. If you marry her, you'll have the right to the throne, and I believe there are men in this very city who would support your claim."

"We've been through all of this before," replied Eric, bored. "You should start writing novels, Laura. You have a talent of making things up." He found his shoes and busied himself with tying the shoelaces.

Laura seated herself at the piano and started playing, and for some time, neither said a word, but then she turned suddenly and her eyes flashed with strange fire. In fact, there were so many things strange about her that Eric had lost count. Sometimes she frightened him.

"So you won't listen to reason, will you? That means you'll bear the full consequences. Remember, I tried to warn you!"

"In God's name, what are you talking about? Are you casting spells or something?"

"Oh, yes, I do," she admitted nonchalantly. "You called me the Queen of Elves once, well, I'm her."

"I think you drank too much champagne at dinner," retorted Eric dryly, putting on his shoulder holster. "Good-bye, Laura."

Her mood changed yet again and she asked him with the tone of a perfect hostess, which nearly made him laugh: "Won't you at least drink a cup of coffee before going?"

Chapter 2. Assault in the Dark

It was half past midnight when Eric finally left Laura's apartment. He wasn't too happy about the way things were going between them. He realized only too well that Laura exercised too much influence over him, that she was capricious and totally unpredictable and getting even more so, and that one word from her to Haakon could ruin him.

Every time he left Laura he promised himself it would be his last visit and then she'd slip him a note somehow, only signed with the letter L and he would anticipate their next meeting eagerly.

She was cautious enough never to contact him on his mobile, in case it would fall into the wrong person's hands, and he had always destroyed all her notes, but he was well aware that by now, Isabella was probably not the only one suspicious of their behavior. The one good thing was, he presumed that there was a certain cooling between his lord and Laura.

Haakon, who could never attach himself to any woman for a long time, was probably getting tired of her after all, and she was furious about his marriage plans. She once admitted it herself while talking to Eric. The status quo suited her perfectly, it was only natural that she wouldn't want it disturbed and that's exactly what the conspirators were intending to do.

The very reason Eric was going to attend Michael's wedding was to meet with some Northern officers and discuss the details of the planned military coup which would get Michael out of their way and make Haakon King of Dakstra. Eric didn't believe for a moment Haakon was using that opportunity only to get rid of him, for His Highness his whole future was at stake and he'd use the help of the Devil himself, if necessary, to get the crown.

As for his own marriage to Isabella, the prince had agreed to it a long time ago, something he'd never had done if he had really suspected that Eric actually had any designs on the throne. Not that the latter had made any progress in his courting efforts lately, in fact, he and the princess hardly spoke to each other at all. He didn't really care since his work and political intrigues left him little spare time and it was all occupied by Laura anyway, though his common sense was screaming at him to stop.

Just like tonight, he knew he had to leave early and yet he stayed much longer than his original intentions had been, which could easily raise suspicions, since officially he had just dropped by to bring her two opera tickets sent by His Highness. And yet he stayed there nearly the whole evening.

The night was dark and the only moon to see that night was concealed by the clouds but there were enough street lanterns to light his way to his car, which was parked a bit further from the main entrance of the apartment building. Eric was the only person in the street or so it seemed as he was walking totally absorbed by his own thoughts. The hard sound of a gunshot pierced the air, roughly awaking him out of his reverie.

At the same moment as the sound was repeated, his survival instinct took over and Eric threw himself on the ground looking for cover behind one of the parked cars and only when he tried to retrieve his own ray gun, he discovered that he'd been hit. He hardly could lift his right arm and there was blood pouring out through the hole in his leather jacket, right beneath his shoulder. He managed to pull out his pistol somehow and changing hands, prepared to shoot back when the silence of the night exploded with rapid automatic fire.

In the lantern light, he clearly saw two men on the opposite side of the parking lot with heavy army rifles, one of them sitting on a motor bike, the other standing next to it. Eric could use his left hand nearly as well as his right one and he was sure that he injured one of his attackers, but at that moment the car to his right took a direct hit to its fuel tank and exploded.

As it went up in flames, Eric was thrown on the pavement and lost consciousness for a short time. When he came to his senses, he could hear police sirens in the distance, but coming closer every second. The car on the right was still burning but luckily the one next to it hadn't caught fire yet. Eric felt dizzy and realized that he must have lost quite a bit of blood by now.

His first instinct was to try to get onto his feet and disappear as soon as possible but it was too late. Just as he was trying to sit up, two policemen approached the scene. Eric closed his eyes and sank back to the ground. He understood he could have been dead by now but the second worst thing happened instead. Now he'd have to explain to His Highness just exactly what he'd been doing in the close proximity to Laura's house at that hour of night.

The police officers were quite efficient. They searched Eric, who was pretending to be unconscious, first and when they examined his documents, one of them whistled and called the ambulance while the other busied himself with first aid. Eric chose that moment to come back to life as he couldn't help swearing because the clumsy efforts of the guy in question were causing him a lot of pain.

"You'll be all right, sir," assured him the policeman. "The wound's not dangerous. No bones broken, either. You've just lost a bit of blood. Can you tell me exactly what happened?"

"Do you have something to drink?" asked Eric instead of answering. He was trying to win some time in order to invent a more or less credible story but his brain was foggy and he found that his teeth were clattering. It was a cold night. The second policeman went back to the patrol car and returned with a thermos can of coffee.

By that time, more police arrived and the ambulance was there, too. The doctor insisted that Eric should be taken to hospital, the police wanted him to make a statement and Eric himself sincerely wished to be a thousand miles away from here. He was trying to estimate how long it would take for the news of this attack to reach Haakon. Just as he thought, it didn't take long.

Less than an hour later he was lying in a hospital bed and telling his story to a police inspector, a middle-aged guy with a shrewd face expression. Eric had decided to restrict his narration to the most essential details concerning his attackers, hoping that the inspector wouldn't ask him what exactly he had been doing in Orchid Street. At that moment, there was a knock at the door but before he could answer, it opened and His Highness stepped inside, with two bodyguards behind him.

The police inspector jumped to his feet and Eric was going to follow his example when Haakon stopped him.

"No, no, stay where you are, Eric! You need rest and quiet. I just thought it was a good idea to check on you personally as to make sure you are all right."

"I am, more or less," replied the latter. "Inspector Thorsten has nearly finished taking down my statement."

Thorsten bowed his head in acquiescence. "I'll come back tomorrow," he said sensing the tension in the room. "In the meanwhile, Colonel, it appears best to me to leave you with police protection in case there will be another assassination attempt."

"It won't be necessary, Inspector. My own private guards will ensure that Colonel Ericsson stays safely in his bed," stated the prince significantly.

Thorsten muttered something unintelligible, bowed and disappeared. Haakon dismissed the bodyguards with a gesture and installing himself on the chair vacated by Thorsten looked at Eric closely.

"Now that we are alone I want to know exactly what happened."

Eric opened his mouth, closed it and opened again and at that moment there was a commotion in the corridor, he heard a shrill female voice talking angrily, then the door burst open and Laura entered the room.

"Your men tried to prevent me from going in," she said, her eyes flashing. His Highness shrugged his shoulders.

"Then they were just following my orders."

"You forget that I'm not one of your subjects, Haakon," retorted Laura haughtily. "And I wouldn't insist on seeing you if I hadn't some darn good reasons, either."

She suddenly appeared to look taller and Eric had to admit that her arrogance was at least equal to that of the prince. Haakon stood up slowly and bowed, half mockingly, half seriously.

"What is this urgent business that brings you here at this time of night, Lady Laurentia?"

Laura pointed to Eric. "I asked Colonel Ericsson to stay longer than he had originally intended as I wanted to ask him a couple of questions…which he chiefly refused to answer. The assassins knew exactly where to find him, which means that they either shadowed him or kept an eye on the apartment building, or both. When shooting first started, I looked out of the window and I believe I can describe the attackers very well. Is that not an important piece of information?"

Both men were silent, so Laura continued: "Furthermore, though the colonel wouldn't tell me what I wanted to know I had heard all about his mission from other sources and I believe that the assassination attempt was undertaken to prevent him from going to Troon and that's some very serious business, indeed."

Haakon's piercing blue eyes fixed themselves on Laura's face. "What exactly are you trying to insinuate?"

"I am not insinuating anything. Except that there is probably someone in your inner circle who can't be fully trusted."

She stared right back at him and wouldn't avert her eyes. His Highness was the first to do so.

"This is hardly the place to discuss such things," he remarked coldly. "And Colonel Ericsson needs his rest. You'd better come with me, Laura. And as for you, Eric, tomorrow we'll transfer you back to the palace. Your wound's not dangerous and you can just as well stay in bed in your own apartment as in the hospital. Good-bye."

"Your Highness, Lady Laurentia," said Eric sitting up and bowing his head. The prince and Laura left and he sank back in bed. He suddenly realized just how terribly tired he was. Before he could determine for himself whether Haakon had believed Laura's story, he fell asleep.

Chapter 3. Some Would Call It Blackmail

Eric was dreaming. He was in the prison camp, running a high fever. A guard came along and started kicking him, telling him to get back to work.

"Bloody bastard!" shouted Eric in reply. "I hope I have the plague so we both die!" At that moment he opened his eyes and realized that he was in his own bed with a splitting headache and that the person trying to wake him up was actually Isabella.

"What the hell are you doing here?" he asked disregarding all rules of decorum. The clock on the wall showed that it was 5 p.m.

Isabella looked offended. "Since I've recently become my brother's nurse of choice, he sent me to check that everything was in order, but really, I wanted to talk to you myself. You've made a pretty mess out of everything, Eric Ericsson!"

"Do we have to discuss it now?" he groaned. "After all, it's not like I committed High Treason or something."

"Well, I'm afraid my brother sees it in a different light."

"He doesn't even love her anymore!"

The princess shook her head. "It's not about love, it's just that you dared to raise your eyes to something that belongs to him, that he considers his property, do you understand? And it also gives him grounds to suspect you of wishing more. In short, my brother assumes you want to become the next king."

Eric sat up. When Laura was talking about the same thing he didn't care, but coming from Isabella, it was serious.

"You don't mean it! He can't accuse me of anything, he has no proof…"

"He doesn't need any. It's not like he wants you to stand trial, you know. Have you asked yourself who it was tried to murder you? Police still have no clue, after hours of investigating."

"Can I have some water, please?" asked Eric. He wasn't feeling much better and the headache prevented him from thinking clearly. She went away and returned with a full glass.

"Who else can be behind it?" inquired Isabella.

"Well, someone in his inner circle who works for the enemy, as Laura suggested."

"They only have to wait three more weeks before you come to Troon, where they can easily get rid of you if they are so inclined, why risking an assassination attempt in Angharad?"

"Then it could be someone who wouldn't want me to go to Troon in the first place, pondered Eric.

"His Excellency wouldn't stoop so low, I'm sure," retorted the princess indignantly. "Not even to promote his nephew's career. By the way, did you know that Wiggles appears to be in love with Laura?"

"Half of all the young officers are in love with her," said Eric indifferently.

"Why did you stay so long in her apartment?"

"She asked me to. She was trying to persuade me not to go to Troon, by the way. Said it was too dangerous."

"Well, there is your answer!" exclaimed Isabella. "She did it all on purpose."

Eric placed the empty glass on a side table and sighed. The last thing he wanted was to discuss politics with Isabella, or anyone else for that matter, but he appeared to have no choice.

"I've had my suspicions about her all along," continued the princess, "but now I'm sure. Laura is a spy."

"A what? You must be kidding."

"Oh no, I'm not," Isabella assured him.

"It's a serious accusation," said Eric slowly.

"Think for yourself. My brother picked her up about two years ago, during an unofficial visit to Troon. She was an exotic singer and dancer, wildly popular, but she had just appeared in the North several months before. Nobody knew exactly where she'd come from or who she was. She has a breeding, everyone can see that, and arrogance befitting a queen, and she's well-educated, too."

"I believe she belongs to the Royal Family of Jokusfelt," replied Eric, "though I could be mistaken."

"A Princess of Jokusfelt? The one who disappeared under such strange circumstances? How do you know? Did she tell you?" Isabella's eyes opened wide.

"No, she didn't tell me anything. I have my reasons for thinking this. I also believe that you hate her because you are jealous."

Isabella blushed. "You have a darn high opinion of yourself, don't you? I could care less about your women, but concerning Laura, the situation's quite different. As I was trying to tell you, no one had any idea about whom or what she was, but she met my brother and he fell for her, hook, line and sinker. He brought her over here and treated her in a way he'd treated no other woman. I believe, especially in the beginning, he shared all his secrets with her. She enjoyed his full confidence, but he never gave her that much money, simply because he didn't have it. He paid her apartment and provided for her, gave her some jewelry and that was it. Yet, the diamond ring alone which she wears costs a fortune, and she didn't get it from him. She also disappears from time to time, under the guise of visiting relatives in the North, yet who these relatives are, nobody knows. Since my brother's affections cooled a bit, she started keeping more or less an open house, organizing musical evenings and stuff like that, all within decency boundaries, of course, as not to make him overtly jealous, but I know very well it's not him who sponsors it all. She must have another source of income. Plus, she knows too much about what's going on. High state officials visit her and they talk about politics. Now you tell me, why would a woman in her position be interested in politics at all?"

Eric was silent. He couldn't help remembering his own encounters with Laura and the questions she would ask now and then, mostly when he least expected it. And his own answers. If Isabella was right, it was bad business.

Some of his thoughts must have reflected upon his face, and the princess smiled bitterly.

"You talked to her about confidential topics, didn't you?"

This time it was Eric who blushed. "These are just your suspicions, nothing else!"

"Deep inside you must know I'm speaking the truth," insisted Isabella. "You swore an oath of allegiance to my house, and you are in charge of security matters in this palace. It's your duty to see to it that she doesn't escape the punishment she deserves."

For a moment Eric had a vision of Laura walking across a prison yard with a blindfold and a target on her chest and he felt slightly nauseous.

"You realize, do you," he said speaking slowly and distinctly, "that I'm hardly in a position to bring charges against Laura without…"

"Without implicating yourself, you want to say?"

He nodded.

"You should have thought about it before," retorted Isabella. "But I don't want your death, Eric, because…because we've been friends for a long time. Yet, I'm convinced that woman is dangerous and it's my duty to my country to unmask her and if you want to prove your loyalty, you will have to help."

"All I have are your assertions, which may or may not be true," he insisted.

"Well, then I suggest we look for proof together and if we find it…You'll know what to do."

"How are you planning to do that?" inquired Eric.

"We'll just go to her apartment tonight and search it."

"I believe you are crazy," said Eric. "First of all, your brother has placed guards in front of my door. Second, you forget that I happen to have a hole in my arm. Third, how are we going to do it?"

"Our rooms are on the same level, and there is a parapet going along the wall, so if you just climb out of the window and walk to my room, we can leave the palace unnoticed. Furthermore, your wound's not dangerous. You can even use your arm a bit. An extra morphine shot will take care of the pain. You won't need to overtly exert yourself. Laura will be at the Opera tonight, with my brother, Lord Vernone and Theodosius, she won't be back until 2 a.m. And as for breaking in, am I wrong to suggest that you have your own key?"

"I'm allergic to morphine," replied Eric gloomily. "It gives me headaches. I don't want to overuse it, you know. The stuff is addictive."

"I think half past midnight is a reasonable time, don't you?" said Isabella cheerfully. "It'll give you enough time to rest after dinner. And then, hopefully, we'll settle the matter of Lady Laurentia once and for all."

Chapter 4. Laura's Secret Life

It was quarter past midnight when Eric finally climbed into Isabella's room. Normally he would have been thrilled to visit her in the dead of night, but not now. He had a good sense of balance and wasn't afraid of heights and it was only the first floor anyway so walking along the palace wall on a narrow parapet wasn't supposed to be particularly strenuous for him, but he still didn't feel well at all and more so, he was considerably angry. The whole idea was preposterous and the way Isabella dragged had him into it tasted of blackmail. In short, he was in the lousiest mood imaginable.

He sprung off the windowsill, making a wrong movement in the process and suppressing a groan, looked around. It was darker in the room than outside and it took him some time to get accustomed to it. It was the first time he visited the private quarters of the princess. She had left the window half-open so he wouldn't have any trouble getting in but she wasn't there herself.

It was a spacious living-room, with a thick carpet on the floor, paintings on the walls and comfortable chairs and Eric sank into one of them with a sigh of relief. At that moment, the adjacent door opened and Isabella came inside. She was dressed in a dark gray two-piece, with a skirt slightly shorter than what she usually wore, falling only a couple of inches below the knee, her long blond hair in a knot.

Eric looked at his own old jeans, sweater and sneakers he had picked up for the occasion and shook his head.

"We are not going to a concert," he said disapprovingly.

"I'm not planning on climbing out of the windows," retorted the princess.

"How do you know? You never told me how you were planning to get there. I can't walk that distance."

"Never mind," said Isabella. "There are some men in this palace who still honor the memory of my father."

"I'm happy to hear that," lied Eric. He wasn't happy at all. "And now listen, Bell, the only reason I agreed to go along with this

130

harebrained scheme of yours is to prove how wrong you are. You've always hated Laura, but this is the limit – you are trying to frame her for espionage, the crime which carries the maximum penalty."

Isabella laughed bitterly. "Save your breath, Eric. We are not in court. The only reason you agreed to go with me is because deep down inside you know I may be right and it scares you. You want to prove the opposite to yourself just as much as you want to prove it to me."

Eric didn't reply. He realized by this time that arguing any further was of no use anyway and the sooner the matter was over and done with, the better. Isabella was pretty determined; he was too, and the time was short.

"Well?" he asked.

"Wait here," said the princess. She disappeared but came back in a couple of minutes.

"Everything is in order. Follow me."

Eric did without asking any questions. They left the room and went through a dusky corridor. When Eric looked back he could just make out two dark figures by his door. He wondered what would happen if they stumbled upon someone. It wasn't that late, after all. He didn't have to wonder long as Isabella touched one of the panels in several places and it slid back leaving an opening the size of a door. Isabella quickly stepped inside with Eric following her. It was a long, narrow, dark passage but Isabella turned a switch and a dim light came from the ceiling.

"No need to break your neck," she remarked. They proceeded along for some time, had to descend a steep staircase, then went round the corner and finally the princess stopped in front of a wall which was exactly like all the others and knocked three times. It slid open and they found themselves in a small dark room somewhere on the ground floor. A tall dark-haired man stood in front of them, with his face covered by a strip of dark fabric. He bowed to Isabella and nodded to Eric.

"Here you are, Your Highness." His voice sounded muffled but strangely familiar. "Two passes for leaving the palace and coming back again. My men will be on duty till 3 o'clock and they won't ask any questions. Mind you destroy them both afterwards. The car will be waiting for you at the Longstreet Corner. Here are the keys. Leave it in the same place when you come back."

"Thank you, my friend," said Isabella. "Your help has truly been inestimable. But what about the agents by the building itself?"

"They are my men, too."

During this conversation Eric was trying to figure out who this mysterious person could be and one name kept popping in his mind.

"No, it can't be true," he said to himself. "And yet…"

"Well, that's settled then," said the princess with an air of satisfaction about her.

"Let's go, Eric."

"I take it we aren't leaving by the main entrance?" he asked and found that his own voice sounded sharper than he had intended.

"No," replied the stranger. "You'll get out by the garden gate. It's half past midnight, so you don't have much time left. Hurry up and good luck."

They didn't have any trouble with following his instructions. The guards at the gate didn't ask them any questions and the car was parked where it should have been. It was a small blue 2-door model, the one often driven by women and not bound to attract much attention. Eric automatically checked the license plate though he was sure it would be changed the next day. Angharad numbers, just as he had expected.

"Your friend has thought of everything." There was an unmistakably mocking intonation in Eric's voice. He couldn't help it. The whole situation was getting on his nerves, especially the role he was forced to play.

"Yes, didn't he?" Isabella hopped into the driver's seat and turned the key.

"I'm glad at least one of us is enjoying himself," remarked Eric taking the seat next to her.

It was ten minutes to one when they finally found themselves in front of the door of Laura's apartment. Eric was still breathing heavily from climbing the stairs. They both agreed that it was probably safer than taking the elevator but later he regretted it. He steadied his hand, turned the key and pushed the door open. He'd done it so many times before, but under different circumstances.

Laura's apartment had a living-room, two bedrooms, a kitchen and a bathroom and was rather a spacious one.

"So where are we going to look first?" he asked in a coarse whisper.

"In her bedroom," replied Isabella, also in a whisper. "That's where I would hide anything of importance. But wait, put on these gloves first."

She took two pairs of latex gloves out of her pocket, handed one to him and pulled on the other one.

"Now we can start searching."

They did their best while trying to leave as few traces as possible, using two electric torches for light. Isabella methodically went through all the drawers, wardrobes, linen closets and even cooking pans. The looked in the bathroom and in the hall. They found her checkbook and bank papers which didn't reveal anything incriminating at all. The big clock in the living-room was ticking and its hands crept ever closer to two. They both sat on the sofa in the living-room in exasperation.

"Well, what will you say now?" inquired Eric, not bothering to check the triumph in his voice.

"We should have taken more time, that's what," retorted Isabella. "We simply didn't have enough time to look everywhere."

"There's no way I'm doing it again," declared Eric. He kicked against the carpet angrily, and it moved. There was nothing special about it, of course, yet there had been a strange hollow sound which they both heard. Eric stomped his foot at the same place again and the sound repeated. In a second, they were both kneeling on the floor looking for a way to remove a timber board.

Eric used his pocket knife and it gave way easily, revealing a hiding place which was stuffed with papers and banknotes, a considerable sum in Northern dollars. Eric counted money mechanically, then took the first envelope from the pile. It was a bank report from a Northern bank. He looked at it and whistled. Laura had a bank account in the North and she was getting substantial sums of money transferred to it monthly, from an anonymous source.

He gave the papers to Isabella, and searched further. The very next thing was a security report which had gone missing last week. It was found three days later. Here, right in front of his eyes, lay a copy of it.

"Good God in Heaven," said Eric and it sounded like swearing. "Good God in Heaven." Meanwhile Isabella pulled out her mobile and started snapping pictures. At that crucial moment they suddenly heard footsteps approaching the apartment door and two people laughing, a man and a woman, and then the sound of the key turning in the lock. For a second, they both were paralyzed, then Isabella grabbed the copy of the report out of Eric's hand, stuffed all the papers into the hole in the floor not caring much about any semblance of order, and pushed the plank back into its place.

It fell in with a click, and Eric coming out of his temporary stupor, pulled the carpet back and taking the princess by the hand, dragged her to the balcony door. Laura's balcony extended beyond the living-room to the kitchen where it was connected to the fire escape. The door had hardly closed behind them as Laura entered the room together with a young officer. Crouched on the floor, Eric looked up and recognized him. It was Lieutenant Wiggles, Archbishop Theodosius's nephew.

Chapter 5. Cousins and Rivals

Had Laura chosen to switch on the light she would have surely noticed them both, but she contended herself with only a small lamp on the side table. Eric felt the princess squeezing his hand and his own heart leaped when he saw Laura going in their direction, but she merely drew the curtains together without paying much attention to what was going on outside, and then proceeded to do the same at the other window, the one facing the street.

Eric could see the silhouettes of both her and the young Wiggles and hear their laughter. Isabella pulled his hand and pointed down. It was evident she desired to leave as soon as possible but Eric still lingered, unable to take his eyes away from the scene in front of him. A champagne bottle was opened, there was more laughter and clicking of glasses. Then Laura said: "To the success of your mission, Lieutenant!"

"Are you sure, your ladyship, that I will get the job, then?" inquired Wiggles.

"Well, obviously Colonel Ericsson won't be able to travel for some time, so after we've finished the champagne I want you to be a good boy, Raymond, and go and tell your uncle…"

The voices became softer as the two moved further away from the balcony. Eric looked at his watch mechanically. Half past two. It was high time they returned to the palace and he was back in bed. His forehead was burning as his fever returned. Trying to make as little noise as possible, they crept to the fire escape and Eric climbed over the railing and helped the princess do the same.

They went down the steep ladder, than another one…Nobody said a word. When they finally found their car and Isabella started the engine, she pressed the gas pedal all the way into the floor, not caring much that they could be stopped for speeding. She drove through the empty streets with complete silence on both sides. They were just in time as the clock struck 3 a.m. when they were entering the palace.

Nobody was waiting for them and they proceeded back to the princess's room where Eric fell into a chair. Isabella didn't turn on the light, she just stayed there looking at him.

"What now?" she asked finally.

"You were right, Your Highness," said Eric furiously, not bothering to temper his voice. "Is that what you wanted to hear, Bell? You were right!"

She came closer and touched his forehead. "You are sick," she said and there was no triumph in her voice. You'd better go to bed immediately. We'll talk tomorrow."

"This report," continued Eric not listening to her. "It went missing. Only several high officials knew about its existence. I was one of them. I swear to God she didn't get it from me, but for your brother it will be enough proof of my guilt. He can't make her stand trial and he never will, but as for myself, it's quite a different thing. But maybe, just maybe, he'll be charitable enough to dispose of me privately. Will you go to him now? The sooner it's over and done with, the better!"

Isabella was biting on her lip. "Eric," she said finally. "I want to make you an offer. No, say nothing, listen to me first! It's not a secret to me that you hate my brother and that you probably have a good reason for it, too. I know it was revenge more than anything that brought you here. Haakon is pragmatic in extreme, devoid of all sentiment. He is my brother so I have few illusions about his true nature.

"He uses people and then discards them when he doesn't need them anymore or when they start getting too dangerous. He is like that to everyone. Look what he's done to me, his own sister! His only emotion is his ambition and Laura is the only woman he's ever really cared for. But then you came and you took her away. He'll never forgive you which means that your life is in danger even now, as I am speaking, so why not taking a gamble?"

Eric straightened himself. "What do you mean?" he inquired coarsely.

136

"There are men in this very palace who are loyal to the House of Angharad but have as little love for Haakon as you do. You met one of them tonight. They'll rally behind me, behind us. If you just stretch your hand, the crown will be yours for taking. You know the law forbids the woman to rule in her own right but if I marry you afterwards, it'll only add more weight to your claim. You have Drakenvuur blood in your veins, you are one of us. You'll make a good king!"

Eric was silent. For a moment, the temptation was almost too much to bear and he nearly succumbed to it, but something stopped him. Was it his pride? He wouldn't rule by the leave of a woman. Or was it something else? He felt like awakening from a dream when he looked the princess straight in the eye and said slowly: "Your offer is very attractive, Your Highness, but I regret to tell you that I'm obliged to refuse it."

Isabella was astonished. "But why, Eric? Why? I don't understand…"

"No wonder," he said rising up. "You are, after all, a woman, Bell, though you can be as hard as nails. However, I swore an oath of allegiance to your brother. I won't dishonor my name by breaking it."

"He'll have you executed for High Treason."

"He probably won't," replied Eric tiredly. "After all, he still needs me. But I'll take my chance. And now I have to leave you. It's high time I was in bed, Good-night, sweetheart, and thanks for thinking of me."

As he was walking along the parapet the princess put her head out of the window and whispered angrily: "I hate you, Eric Ericsson."

He didn't answer, afraid to lose his balance as he was really feeling quite horrible. It took him only a couple of minutes to change into his pajamas and then he finally reached his bed and was asleep in a moment, despite pain and fever.

Left to his own devices, Eric would have probably slept the whole morning, but at 9.30 a.m. he was woken up by Isabella who looked pale and had dark circles under her eyes like one who hadn't slept the whole night.

"Laura has disappeared," she announced. "Nobody knows where she is but the rumor spread she's gone up North. She probably noticed the disarray in her papers last night. My brother will be here any moment." Eric didn't answer.

She checked his bandages, brought him a cup of tea and toast with marmalade. Despite the adventures of last night Eric was feeling better. He devoured his breakfast and went into the bathroom to dress and shave. Isabella looked despondent when he finally came out.

"What are we going to do?"

"We'll tell him the truth," said Eric. "It's just that simple."

He went back to bed, pulled his blanket up to his chin and tried to think, but the only thought that kept popping up in his mind was the realization that Laura was now lost to him forever and that it was his own fault, too. His and the woman sitting close to him, watching him anxiously. He could control his emotions just as well as anyone else but it had never before taken him such a tremendous effort to conceal his rage and his disappointment and that hollow sense of loss.

"He'll never forgive me," thought Isabella. It was at this moment that His Highness entered the room. Eric sat up and said in a low but steady voice: "My lord, I'm going to make a statement…"

"So that's it, then," concluded the prince. "And you, dear sister, support Ericsson's testimony, don't you?"

She nodded and showed him the photos on her mobile.

"Well, that explains a lot of things," pondered Haakon. "A lot of things, except one. How did you get inside the apartment?"

Eric rose up and looked at his rival. "I've got the key," he replied. Isabella gasped in horror and put her hand to her mouth. The two men kept staring at each other with flashing eyes and Eric wouldn't lower his as the palace etiquette demanded.

"You can use your left hand just as well as you right one, as far as I know," said Haakon finally. Eric nodded. The princess jumped to her feet. "You can't fight with him, brother. You can't! It won't be fair! He's wounded!"

"He should have thought of it before," answered His Highness coldly. "I'll be in the Royal Hall, Eric. Don't keep me waiting." He turned and left.

Eric put his shoes on and took his polariton sword out of the drawer where he usually kept it. He switched it on and off and smiled in grim satisfaction.

"He'll kill you," said the princess with a note of despair in her voice. "He's awfully good at it. Practices every day. And you aren't feeling well and you'll have to fight with your left hand."

"Get out of my way, Isabella," he retorted pushing her aside. "Isn't that what you wanted all the time?" and with these words he went out of the room.

They were just the two of them in a spacious and empty Royal Hall and there were no words wasted. From the very first moment that they crossed their blades Eric knew that his adversary was going for a kill. He had sparred with Haakon before and was well aware that his own skills were inferior to the prince's, especially now that he felt so weak and tired and had to use his left hand. But his fury and his despair gave him an unusual strength and he was determined to sell his life dearly.

Haakon, who had expected an easy victory, was taken by surprise and made a couple of mistakes but quickly regained the lost ground. They both got a couple of insignificant scratches but Eric had already lost a lot of blood and tiredness was finally catching up with him. He knew he couldn't go on like this much longer. There was cold sweat on his forehead and a strange ringing in his ears and red mist in front of his eyes which was getting thicker.

The prince who had been watching him closely, seized his opportunity: with a swift movement he sent Eric's sword flying through the air, the next second his own blade was at Eric's throat.

"You won't beg me for your life, will you, cousin?" he inquired, still breathing heavily. Eric only shook his head. He was unable to speak. Suddenly His Highness switched off his sword.

"I want you to remember this encounter, Eric," he said significantly. "I want you to always remember that you can't win over me. And by God, you'd better succeed on that diplomatic mission to Troon!"

"I'll do my best, cousin," replied Eric smiling wanly.

The prince swore. "You are as arrogant as…"

"As my father?" asked Eric.

"As any damned Drakenvuur," stated Haakon. "Welcome to the family!"

Chapter 6. Curiosity Killed the Cat

Four weeks later Eric was standing inside the main cathedral of Troon which was at least one thousand years old and looking around with interest. The ancient cathedral was full as all the high officials of the North and a preselected number of commoners occupied all the pews.

Young and old, male and female, all the faces were turned to the altar where His Eminence Cardinal Reginus officiated a marriage sermon, The Right Reverend Father Bishop Theodosius standing next to him. Derek White sat in the first row, while Eric himself was standing among security staff, in a position which allowed him a good view of the whole building.

He had been offered a front seat as well, but chose to decline it as he preferred to have freedom of movement. Two of his men were situated behind him, the two others were placed on the other side of the church. They were a small delegation, but then nobody really expected His Excellency to be in any kind of danger.

Eric looked at the bride: a young girl not older than 19 who appeared positively scared; her lips trembling. Michael wasn't particularly ugly but he was known to have fits of rage and overall, a rather unpleasant personality. Eric felt sympathy with the girl, but only for a moment as his thoughts became distracted by other things.

There were some officers present, of the security, of the palace guards, the high army commanders, all in gala uniforms, as opposed to himself. Again, he chose civilian clothes to attract less attention, citing his bodyguard duties. Were the coup leaders in the church as well? The instructions given to him were vague enough: he had to be present at the wedding and then further contact would be established.

Meanwhile, the wedding liturgy was trailing on, the rings were exchanged, the nuptial blessings given. Cathedral bells rang merrily. It was now time to return to the palace for the reception, and later, dinner.

Eric found his way to the main entrance and stood there for several minutes, examining those who were going out. There was a moment when the crowd really pressed on him and it was then that he felt someone grabbing him by the hand and pushing something into it. A note! He was sure it was one but he wasn't as sure as to who had given it to him, there were so many people trying to get out at the same time.

He finally found himself outside, a piece of paper firmly clutched in his right hand. Realizing it was hardly a place to read it, he put it in his pocket, but he had to wait till the reception was over to learn its contents.

"So they contacted us," stated Derek with satisfaction. Their rooms were adjacent and they shared a balcony, the only place they deemed safe for the confidential discussions even though they had combed both of their rooms the evening before searching for spyware. "What now? Are you going there?"

"Of course, I am," answered Eric lazily. "That's why I'm here, after all."

"It could be dangerous," pondered Derek. "Should I go with you?"

"I'd rather have you stay behind and cover my back. If something happens to me, you'll probably be able to get me out of it, but if something happens to both of us…"

"I see your point. But take care!"

"I always do, don't I?" laughed Eric quietly. "Remember they call me the lucky one?"

Derek White shrugged his shoulders. He didn't share his friend's "the Devil may care" attitude, and he really didn't understand what possessed Eric of late, that is, unless the palace gossips were right and there had been something between him and that witch Laura. He had never really liked her. Derek White had thoroughly square tastes in women. They had to be virtuous, pleasant and decorative, occupied with charity work and other feminine pursuits, not with political and love intrigues. But then, some men liked it hot and Eric was obviously one of them.

The note was short and to the point. It simply stated: 5 o'clock at the Art Hall, second entrance left, and that's where Eric arrived a quarter of an hour earlier than the designated time.

The Royal Palace of Troon where they were staying, was huge, much bigger than the one in Angharad, with many corners, nooks, entrances, corridors, mysterious passages, spacious halls and all of it was richly decorated and produced an overall fairy tale impression. It was also heavily mortgaged to help pay for the costs of war, with the Uranians holding the purse strings.

Eric looked around curiously trying to imprint all the details of his surroundings in his memory though he doubted it could help him much. As the big clock struck five, he approached the second entrance left and saw a young man with blond hair, dressed in the dark blue uniform of the palace guards. He looked at Eric significantly, nodded, and went out of the door with Eric following him at a distance.

They entered a narrow corridor, turned left, went through a small room with a huge fireplace, entered another passage, even more narrow and dark; turned right and had to descend the stairs. There his guide stopped and for the first time addressing Eric informed him that he'd have to be blindfolded if he desired to proceed further. Eric didn't care for it in the slightest but seeing that he had little choice nodded in agreement.

His guide, still not satisfied with this safety measure, turned him around several times, after which Eric lost all sense of direction. His ray gun was taken from him, too, and he was now totally at the mercy of the stranger, who took him by the hand and guided him through corridors and staircases into the great unknown.

After what seemed a fairly long time, they finally reached their destination, the blindfold was taken off and Eric found himself in a small square room without windows, apparently situated somewhere in the palace basement. It was scarcely lit by LED lamps in the ceiling and contained a table, several chairs, an old-fashioned cupboard and a couch. Three men were sitting around the table, all in civilian clothes; two about Eric's age and one slightly older. He was obviously the one in charge.

"Thank you, Mike," he said in a thick Northern accent, and the guide bowed and left. Eric stood blinking, waiting for his eyes to get accustomed to light again.

"Please, sit down, Colonel Ericsson," continued the man. He had gray eyes, dark brown hair and dark beard and looked about forty.

"My name is Peterson. Colonel Peterson from the Royal Northern Air Force. My two friends prefer to stay unnamed, to lessen the risks of detection, but one of them occupies a high position in State Security while the other one is of the Palace Guards. We don't have much time, so let's get down to business."

Eric shook hands with all three men wondering at himself for doing so. Politics made strange bed fellows indeed!

"I presume you are representing the Royal Power in Angharad?" inquired Peterson. Eric showed his ring instead of an answer and asked in his turn: "How do I know you are the person I'm supposed to meet?"

"That's how!" Peterson shoved a card across the table, it was the king of hearts with its face eerily resembling Michael and the ancient rune of death written over it. He took out a big hunting knife and pierced the image. Though he recognized the sign, Eric shuddered in spite of himself, for a moment it looked to him as if blood came out of the place where the blade had pierced the paper. It must have been an optical illusion of some sorts.

"The South doesn't want his death," he stated, "but he'll have to go into exile. The less blood shed, the better our public image will be." Peterson nodded in agreement.

"I'd like to see the bastard's head on the chopping block," interrupted the man on his right.

"Don't we all," said Peterson coldly, "but we have to be pragmatic if we wish for success. And we have to act quickly, there is no time to lose…"

It took them more than an hour to discuss all the details, as Peterson wanted the guarantees for himself and his comrades. There would be full amnesty for everyone involved in fighting on the other side, no retributions of any kind, no political persecution, the basic rights and freedoms restored, the officials willing to swear allegiance to the new government would keep their positions while those against it would join Michael in exile. Eric agreed to all these demands but pointed out that Reginus would have to go.

"His Eminence is one of the pillars of the current regime. Besides, he's getting too old. It's time for change," he declared. Peterson wasn't entirely convinced of the propriety of this course of action but had to give in in the end. Eric briefly thought of what Lord Ravencroft would say had he heard him shilling for Theodosius like that, but dismissed the concerns. His stepfather and himself would probably never see eye to eye on anything. The conspirators didn't reveal exact details of the coup but promised that they would strike within the next three months.

"It's now or never," declared Peterson, and both his companions agreed. Either of them had hardly said a word during the whole length of the negotiations but now they started talking at once, expressing their full support of the plan. They looked very much like brothers, both athletically built, sun-burned, blue-eyed and blond and indeed, Eric learned later that they were.

When the talks were over, Mike reappeared and brought Eric back to the Art Hall, with the same precautions. It was half past six, high time to change for dinner which would begin in an hour, so he briefly informed Derek about the success of their mission and went back to his room. Only now did he realized how tired he was. The dinner was a long, boring event and though Eric kept his eyes open searching for his new acquaintances, they were apparently not invited.

It was after 10 p.m. when he returned and the first thing he saw lying on the table was a white envelope with no name on it. Curious, Eric opened it and his heart skipped a bit: it was a note in Laura's hand-writing. It said: "Midnight at the Southern Gate and don't tell anyone. Yours always."

Eric debated the matter in his mind. He knew he probably shouldn't go but his common sense couldn't win against his desire to see her again, one last time. After all, what could happen to him now, he reasoned. He'd just go for a walk, besides, they were not prisoners in the palace and Troon was basically safe at night. He would have done the same had it been utterly unsafe, but he wouldn't admit it.

The Southern Gate opened into one of the main streets of the city, but the part of it close to the palace was empty at that hour. It was May and the chestnut trees were blossoming. The whole atmosphere was that of romance and Eric's heart was beating faster than usual. He saw a shadow coming out from behind a tree, looking like a woman, tall and slender, wrapped in a long cloak. She beckoned him to follow her and he did, like one enchanted.

As he was approaching the tree, another figure appeared. The realization that it had been a trap came too late as it raised its hand with a stun gun in it. The next thing Eric knew was that he was lying on the ground incapacitated and a man bent over him with a dark object in his hand. The barrel of a pistol came down upon his head as a ton of bricks and Eric slipped into utter darkness.

Chapter 7. The Prince of Darkness

When he came to, suffering from a splitting headache, he found himself lying on a dirty mattress in a dimly lit room without windows which reminded him of medieval dungeons and was probably one, too. He heard the sound of running water, but no other sounds reached him. Eric wondered how long he had been unconscious. The wedding, his meeting with the conspirators, Southern Gate…it all seemed to have happened ages ago. In fact, it had been only several hours, as he realized later.

His first attempt to rise on his feet was not successful and ended with him falling back on the mattress overcome by nausea and dizziness, but the second attempt went better and he managed to sit up with his back to the wall and look around. There was little comfort in what he discovered.

First of all, his hands were shackled with old-fashioned chains which allowed him a certain freedom of movement but were heavy and inconvenient. The walls were made of massive stones and looked if they were a couple of meters thick at the very least while the floor consisted of stone slabs. It had a grating in the middle and he could see water down below and there was also a pipe sticking out of the wall with a leaky faucet at the end. That was apparently all in the way of sanitary installation that his cell possessed.

Further on there was a massive oak door with metal bars across it and ventilation holes in the ceiling for fresh air. A light bulb was installed in one of them. The dungeon was cold and damp but at least, they had given him a blanket. Eric wrapped himself in it as well as he could and tried to think.

Whoever his kidnappers were, they obviously didn't plan to kill him right away, which was probably for the worse. He remembered the four weeks he had spent in a Uranian prison on Tarna with a shudder. He still had scars on his wrists and on his back. Would he have to go through it again? The idea was horrifying.

At that moment there was some noise behind the door, then it opened and a guard entered the room. It was a young guy not much older than twenty, with red hair, blue eyes and a freckled face. He looked more like a farmer's son than a hangman's assistant. He was dressed all in black but wore no uniform and no insignia of any kind, just black jeans, a black sweater and a black leather jacket, and he carried a stun gun instead of regular weapons.

The guard had a tray in his hands with a cup of coffee and two pieces of toast on it. He could have been a waiter in a village inn. There was such a striking dissonance between his every day appearance and his surroundings that Eric couldn't help laughing. The guard started and nearly dropped his tray.

"Here's your breakfast, sir," he announced, clumsily putting the tray on the ground.

"What's your name?" asked Eric.

"Max, sir."

"Can you tell me where I am?"

"We aren't allowed to talk to prisoners, sir," said the guard and left. Eric shrugged his shoulders. He was still experiencing nausea but coffee made him feel better and he found himself equal to eating jam and toast, too, though he would have preferred bacon and eggs.

After breakfast he washed himself as well as he could, lay down upon his mattress and wondered what was the meaning of all this and whether Max could be persuaded to help. He must have dozed off as some time later he woke up with a start only to find the dungeon door open again. This time there were two men, dressed in the same fashion as Max, but older and carrying army rifles. They told Eric to stand up and get moving, which he did as best as he could since he had to fight dizziness.

They went up the stairs and into a corridor with a window which, as Eric duly noted, was unbarred but the only thing he could see through it was water and the mountains far away. He figured out that he was in some ancient castle situated on an island in a mountain lake. Now, what did it remind him of?

He didn't have much time to think as one of the guards pushed him with the rifle barrel and told him to move on. Another staircase, and then he was ushered into a room, sparsely furnished, with an enormous fire place and an old-fashioned chair standing in the center of it. In fact, it looked much more like a throne than a chair.

A man was sitting in it, in his middle fifties, with dark graying hair and piercing dark eyes. He had dark complexion and there was something in his face which made him resemble a hawk. There was a silver diadem upon his head with a single diamond in the middle. Dressed in a black suit with a white shirt, the stranger produced a powerful impression. Eric was stunned as he suddenly realized who the man in front of him was. It was like a fairy tale come true. No, not a fairy tale, more like a nightmare.

"Allfather," he whispered, "help me, for I'm surely lost this time." Some of his feelings must have reflected upon his face as the man in the chair smiled with satisfaction. Something about that smile made Eric so mad that he suddenly felt defiant instead of horrified.

"Lord Hammerstone, I presume?" he inquired, in the most insolent manner possible. "Charmed to make your acquaintance, my lord."

Lord Hammerstone's eyes flashed, but only for a second. The smile returned onto his thin lips. "Sit down, Colonel Ericsson," and he pointed to another chair, much smaller and at a distance. The guards were dismissed and they were left with just the two of them. Eric tried to figure out whether he could attack his adversary before the guards could be summoned but had to reject the idea.

The distance was too big, his chains were slowing him down considerably and Lord Hammerstone was probably armed as well. There was a long pause during which two men kept watching each other closely, then finally Lord Hammerstone spoke.

"Do you have any idea, Colonel, as to why I wanted to see you?"

"To keep you company during long summer evenings?" asked the latter. "It must be awfully lonely here in the mountains with only local peasants to chat with."

Lord Hammerstone coughed. "I wish you'd be a bit more serious, Colonel, as it's your future which is at stake."

"My future and my life?" wanted Eric to know. The man on the throne nodded solemnly. At that moment he looked so very much like the incarnation of the Prince of Darkness in his own person that Eric, who was superstitious by nature, had to fight against an inclination to bless himself. Lord Hammerstone had such a dreadful reputation that Eric's feelings were hardly surprising.

Eric recalled stories of fair maidens disappearing, of secret dungeons and torture chambers, of satanic rituals taking place under the cover of darkness, of the undue influence His Lordship excercised over Michael, of the horror which his name produced among the local population etc. etc. Surely, all of these stories couldn't be true? And yet, Lord Hammerstone ruled his province more like his own private kingdom and wielded an enormous power in the Northern region. Add to this his tremendous wealth, his strange habits, his appearance, his legendary cruelty and it wasn't a wonder that people believed he had sold his soul to the Devil.

Yet, again Eric's anger was kindled. He wouldn't allow himself to be intimidated by these theatrical tricks, he who had royal blood in his veins, he wouldn't bend his knee to anyone, be it a man or a demon.

"What the Hell do you want from me?" he inquired. "What is the meaning of all this?"

"How would you like to be the next king?" asked Lord Hammerstone. "No, don't say anything, Colonel, but listen to me first. My reputation is probably not a secret to you. Some of the things people say are exaggerated, while others...In short, it was I who facilitated Michael's rise to his current position. However, he disappointed me. Short-sighted and weak-willed, he could not consolidate the gains he'd made and even as we talk, his power is waning.

"He's unpopular among the common folks and he can't trust even his own personal guards, let alone the army as a whole. His demise appears inevitable and it leaves Haakon and yourself as the only two living Drakenvuurs. Haakon made a deal with Delta which I'm afraid, doesn't take into consideration the best interests of Dakstra. I represent the interests of Uranius and my own and I offer you the crown if you swear your personal allegiance to me. The details could be discussed later, the most important thing is whether you agree or not."

"Surely, you can't be serious!" exclaimed Eric.

"Why not?" said his Lordship coldly. "Do you doubt that it lies in my ability? And don't you hate your current lord?"

"And if I refuse?"

"You are an intelligent man, Colonel," stated Lord Hammerstone. "You must understand that in this case, I can't let you live."

"It's not much of a choice really, is it?" said Eric bitterly.

"So you accept, don't you?"

Eric was silent for a moment. He was staring at the floor tiles in front of him, then rose his eyes and looked at his Lordship.

"I swore an oath of allegiance to Haakon," he declared.

Lord Hammerstone's face expression didn't change.

"I'm well aware how stubborn you are, but I hope that when you think the matter over, your common sense will prevail. I'm leaving on some business for three days starting tomorrow. When I come back, I'll hear your answer, Colonel. Guards, take him away!"

And thus Eric was brought back into his dungeon and left alone with his own thoughts, which at that particular moment were far from cheerful.

Chapter 8. An Unexpected Ally

"And so we got engaged last month! But I'm afraid we'll have to wait a long time still for our wedding…" sighed Max.

"It's very unfortunate," agreed Eric. He had spent the better part of the evening getting acquainted with his guard. Max was a simple country guy feeling desperately lonely in that strange ancient castle and Eric had little trouble in making him talk. A plan started forming in his mind, though admittedly rather a vague one.

"There is something I don't understand though," he continued: "How could a loyal son of One True Church join the service of the man who is in league with the Forces of Evil?"

On the other side of the door Max gasped audibly. "But sir," he protested, "after my parents' death, what else could I do? My father left me only debts, I lost the farm and all the family property and still couldn't pay them. And then, there was Marie…

He didn't finish the sentence but jumped to his feet suddenly. "Someone is coming," he announced and then Eric heard light steps and a woman's voice saying, "Open the door."

"My lady," protested Max, "the prisoner is dangerous. You can't visit him alone, like that."

"I said, open the door!" This time there was a sharp note in her voice. She went inside and Eric stood up to greet her. She was wearing a long black dress with a low décolleté and a wide skirt and the color provided a strange contrast to her hair. He had never seen her wear black before.

"You look like a vampire's bride," announced Eric.

"And you look like the bloody idiot you are!" retorted Laura. "How could you fall for such a simple trap?"

"So you didn't write this letter, did you?"

"No," she said emphatically. "In fact, I tried my best to prevent you from ever coming here."

"Were you behind the attempt on my life?" inquired Eric.

"Had I wanted your life, you'd have been dead by now," she replied coldly. "I warned you, too; but you wouldn't listen. You have always been obstinate. Why wouldn't you let Wiggles go instead?"

"Somehow I'm not surprised at meeting you here," said Eric instead of an answer. "So that's your secret, you work for the most loathsome man in the whole Kingdom. You have been his agent all these years, haven't you?"

"My life is my own," declared Laura haughtily. "I'm not obliged to give account of my doings to anyone, least of all to you!"

"Why did you come then?" wondered Eric.

"Because I have a weak spot for you. Hammerstone always does what he says which means that if you don't change your mind in three days you'll be dead."

Eric leaned against the wall. Those chains were pretty uncomfortable.

"Would you miss me?" he inquired.

Laura stamped her foot. "I guess you don't realize the seriousness of your situation! You aren't thirty yet! You have you whole life in front of you! Why would you choose to die just to keep faith with Haakon? He betrayed you once, he'll do it again."

Eric shrugged his shoulders. "Haakon is a politician. He acted in the interests of his country. In his place, I'd probably do the same. Anyway, it's not about him. It's about me."

Laura laughed sarcastically. "You like to talk about your agnosticism but the truth is that you still keep the old superstitions. You believe that oath-breakers will spend eternity in Hell, don't you?"

"Surely, there are better ways to spend the evening than discussing theology?"

"What about your ambition? Restoring your father's bloodline?"

"Believe it or not, I have always been primarily motivated by patriotism," declared Eric. "All other things were secondary to that. As for my father...I'm sure he wouldn't have wanted his only son to dishonor his ancestors by selling his soul for worldly goods."

To his surprise, Laura suddenly sank to the ground. "Are you all right?" asked Eric anxiously, sitting down next to her. "Are you feeling well?"

"I'm perfectly all right, thank you," she responded tiredly. "It's just that you are so darn stubborn, I simply don't know what to do."

"You could help me escape," suggested Eric.

"Escape? You must be out of your mind! How are you planning to do it? The castle is well-guarded, plus it is in the middle of a lake."

Eric lowered his voice. "What have you done to the guard?"

"Told him to wait upstairs for my return. He's afraid of me, the simp. Only's been here for a couple of months."

"Well, I have figured out so much," continued Eric. "He's very religious, too. Kept asking me about His Excellency whom he sees as some kind of a saint."

Laura chuckled. "And, of course, you forgot to tell him that you are both a heretic and an unbeliever, didn't you?"

"The first may be, but not the second. Anyway, that's not the point. The point is that I think he could be persuaded to help."

Laura shook her head. "He is scared out of his wits by Hammerstone. They all are. He may appear sympathetic to your plight, but in the end he'll do as he is told."

"Not if we take him with us."

"We?" Laura raised her eyebrows. "Do you suggest that I go back to the South? After what happened? Being shot for espionage isn't exactly my idea of fun."

"Haakon won't do it."

"He'll have to, to save face. Anyway, even were it otherwise it's still absolutely out of the question."

"It makes things more complicated," pondered Eric. "I can hardly leave you alone over here to face the consequences."

"I can take care of myself, thank you very much," stated Laura coldly. "You'd better think of your own troubles."

Eric shrugged his shoulders. "Well, suit yourself. If you prefer Hammerstone's company to a romantic elopement with me…"

"You are getting insolent," retorted Laura. "I'm severely tempted to leave you to your fate. But then, you can't probably help it, either. You'd keep talking nonsense even with a noose around your neck!"

"Isn't it part of my charm?" inquired Eric. "Anyway, we are wasting time. That guy, Max is his name, lost both his parents in a fire which devastated their family farm which was heavily mortgaged as well. He is engaged to a local girl called Marie who is also an orphan and lives with distant relatives treating her poorly and he took this job with Hammerstone because he saw it as the only way to solve his financial problems and to be able to get married soon. On the other hand, his religious feeling and his conscience keep interfering with his duties. I do believe if he saw another way out he'd quit overnight.

"Add to this his very real fear of Lord Hammerstone who he believes is in league with the Devil and you'll realize he doesn't need much persuasion. I could offer him a job as a security agent with Theodosius, he'd love it. Add to this a sufficient sum of money for the wedding and the problem is solved. He has no family left so Hammerstone won't be able to take revenge on them. The only thing needed is to bring Marie into safety and here is where you come in. You could give her some money and a train ticket to Angharad and tell her to wait there.

"I also need to get rid of these chains, but I think stealing the key is no problem. There is a window upstairs, facing the lake. It's unbarred. Max and I jump out of it and swim to safety. That's Lake Moonlight, isn't it? Once we are on the other side, we'll be close to the border. If you could provide us with a car…"

"Wait a minute," interrupted Laura. "This all sounds plausible enough, except one thing. How are you going to swim so far, with that arm of yours? It's more than two kilometers. You won't be able to do it!"

"I'm fine, really," he responded. "Plus, Max appears to be a darn good swimmer. Has won several swimming competitions. That's what really gave me an idea. Because I think trying to steal a boat is just a waste of time, isn't it?"

"Don't even think of it," warned him Laura. "There are cameras installed and what not. The security will be all over you in a second. No, this swimming plan of yours isn't actually half as crazy as it sounds."

"So you'll help me, won't you?"

She rose to her feet and looked at her watch. "I need to go. It's getting late and my lord Hammerstone hasn't left yet. He'll miss me."

"Does he know you are here?"

"He sort of sent me around to try and make you change your mind," she admitted reluctantly.

Eric stood up and was watching her closely. There was a pause, then she continued:

"You work on Max, if he agrees…We'll see. I'll come again, tomorrow."

He caught her hand and kissed it. "Laura…" he started, but she took her hand away and shook her head.

"Don't say anything, Eric. Better not. Leave it be."

"As you wish, Laura."

She went out and he kept staring at the door for some time, then aroused himself. There was still much work to do.

Chapter 9. A Fresh Start

Max didn't really need much persuading. Before the night was over, he agreed to the plan and now the only thing to do was to work out the details. The next day he had a leave and promised to use it to discuss things with his fiancée. Laura was absent the whole day and Eric started getting nervous even though he wouldn't admit it to himself.

She came in the evening, about the same hour as the day before but stayed just short enough to inform him that their plans were proceeding well. She had met with Max in a remote corner of the village and provided him with an ample sum to make the necessary arrangements. They would use Max's own car which he'd park on the other side of the lake that night and go back by train. She also managed to get hold of the keys and make a duplicate.

"Be ready tomorrow night," she told him and left without giving him an opportunity to thank her. Sunday night the air was cool but the sky was cloudy, with no stars or moon shining. An ideal night for an escape. Eric had had a brief conversation with Max in the morning and learned that Marie had left on the very first train. She'd be in Angharad before the night fell and send her fiancé a message.

At 11 p.m. the door of his dungeon opened and Max came in, with the keys in his hand. It cost him some trouble to open the lock, but finally the chains fell off and Eric breathed a sigh of relief. They climbed the stairs in silence and entered the corridor. A lone figure stood by the window, which was open.

"May Allfather protect you wherever you go, Eric," she said quietly.

He looked at her one last time. "Good-bye, the Elven Queen! One day we will meet again, in this world or the better one."

And so they parted without as much as shaking hands as Eric plunged into the cold water after Max. The next couple of hours required all his concentration and endurance and when they finally reached the shore, he was beyond exhaustion. They made it across the border without much trouble but were stopped by the police somewhere half way to Angharad and it took Eric a lot of trouble to establish his identity.

"But all is well that ends well," he said to Derek White when narrating his adventures. He omitted everything concerning Laura in his report though he wasn't convinced that Haakon really believed him. However, His Highness's thoughts were preoccupied with more important things as his own fate and that of the whole kingdom would be decided within three months, and what was Laura compared to that?

Colonel Peterson held his word and Haakon held his. Six months later, he was proclaimed King of the whole Dakstra which was an exaggeration since there were still the lands of the Northern barbarians more or less independent from the kingdom. It was on the Northern border that the Duchy of Argentson lay and according to the popular rumors it was to the Utter North that Lord Hammerstone escaped to after the coup.

Michael went into exile with his young wife that was by then four months pregnant, some state officials followed him while others chose to swear allegiance to the new king. The secret treaty with Uranius was cancelled and Deltan military arrived on Dakstra in due time, followed by engineers, mining specialists and businessmen.

In January of the year '08, Theodosius was proclaimed Cardinal of Dakstra and in his new role he officiated the wedding ceremony between King Haakon and Princess Freya of Jokusfelt and Eric finally got that one thing he had desired above all: a duke's crown.

"Well, I hope your ambition is finally satisfied," stated Lord Ravencroft when Eric visited him before going to the North. "Just don't think that your new task will be easy. Ruling the whole province is slightly different from organizing revolutions, you know. There is difference in religion as well, though to my knowledge you probably have none."

Eric shrugged his shoulders. "I succeeded in my first endeavor, why shouldn't I succeed in my next one? But then you have never thought highly of my abilities, have you, sir?"

"I know Haakon," stated his stepfather. "I know there is bad blood between you plus the fact that you two are the only Drakenvuurs left. He kept his word to you but secretly he is expecting you to fail. The Duchy of Argentson has been under the Crown rule for thirty years now, but the real master of it for the last decade was Lord Hammerstone. He's been the evil genius behind many plans and you crossed him first, when you refused to serve him, then when you made Haakon king and finally, when you took over the Duchy. He won't forgive and he won't forget.

"He has powerful allies among the Northern barbarians. There is low level guerilla fighting going there since Haakon took power. You'll have to pacify the province and how are you planning to do it? If you are too lax, they'll lose all respect for you, and if you resort to hard measures, they'll hate you for spilling blood. It's a lose-lose situation and His Majesty knows it. That's probably why he agreed to your claims in the first place, because the Duchy is nothing but trouble. The current governor who swore an oath of allegiance to the new king, has been assassinated this very morning!"

"I heard the news," Eric informed him. "I know it's not an easy task. But damn it, my father's line has been ruling this province for ages, why couldn't I?"

"You are not your father. In fact, being illegitimate, you can't even openly proclaim you are his son. In the eyes of the locals you are an accursed Southern invader. I must be much mistaken or there will be attempts on your life as well. That's exactly what Haakon would prefer, that you are out of the way, and not by his hand, either."

"I have long thought that my life is charmed," pondered Eric. "I should have been dead long ago, and yet, here I am. There must be a meaning behind all this. Allfather will be with me wherever I go; besides, I'll be surrounded by friends."

"First an agnostic, now a heathen," stated his stepfather sarcastically. "But you have always been superstitious. As for friends…I'll admit that Lord Vernone agreeing to be your new governor is a tremendous achievement on your part, and I have nothing against Derek White. But that guy you dragged from the North, Max Lain…Why didn't you leave him with Theodosius?"

"Max wanted to be my private bodyguard," said Eric. "What's wrong with that? He's probably just grateful for the chance I've given him. He's married to this girl now and I heard she's expecting."

"Exactly," interrupted Lord Ravencroft. "And he used to work for Lord Hammerstone, too, and Hammerstone doesn't forgive betrayal. He'll always be a weak link, especially now that he's got a family to take care of."

"Max is loyal and brave," retorted Eric, "and I doubt Hammerstone will try to use him against me. That's all settled, anyway. I hoped you'd wish me luck, sir, but I see now that I was quite mistaken."

His stepfather's face darkened. "I do wish you luck, Eric, that's why I was trying to warn you. Your position is still very unstable and you should take steps to secure it. What you need is a heir. Why don't you marry?"

Eric was silent. Lord Ravencroft sighed. "You were planning to marry Isabella, weren't you? So what happened?"

"She probably won't have me. We hardly speak to each other."

"You have always been an idiot in everything concerning women," declared his stepfather. "Of course, she won't talk to you, after your scandalous affair with that foreign harlot."

"That foreign harlot saved my life. As for Bell, I thought you didn't like her, either."

"I've changed my mind about her. She's worth twenty girls like Laura. Eric, believe me, you are making a mistake."

"I'm not in a position to marry right now, the way things are, as there is still much work to do, especially since the previous governor is dead and there is no one to inform Lord Vernone about the true state of affairs; yet with him taking over this function and Derek being the chief of my security I think we can achieve a lot in a short time. However, my real hope lies in the fact that His Eminence promised to visit the Duchy during Easter holidays. His endorsement will carry a great weight with the local population."

"He won't do it for nothing," stated Lord Ravencroft.

"Oh, I know," answered his stepson lightly. "I have no illusions concerning His Eminence. He wants the reversal of the secularization process, complete with the abolishment of the law about the separation of Church and State."

Lord Ravencroft turned red. "Eric, you don't want to tell me you are going to help him achieve this? It's bad enough your intrigues gave him that position of power he doesn't deserve!"

"Theodosius is a snake as ever was one," admitted Eric, "but I'd rather have him as a friend than as an enemy. Delta will never allow the One Church to regain its old power now that they have their collective finger in the pie, so there is nothing to worry about. As for His Eminence's demands, I will negotiate. I'm prepared to go as far as bringing back full religious education in state schools, with the exception for Dissenters, of course; giving extra free days for some religious holidays and subsidizing the building of the new cathedral, but no further, and that won't hurt anyone. And then, if things turn out the way I hope, we'll see…"

He didn't finish his sentence as he suddenly thought of Isabella with a strange kind of longing. What he had told his stepfather was true, he hardly ever spent much time with the princess, in fact, he was still mad at the part she had played in the whole affair with Laura and she always looked offended when she met him, but he knew she was close by and somehow, it was enough. And now they were separated and Heaven only knew when they would get a chance to meet again. He had to admit to himself that he missed her. Not like he missed Laura, but in some way Bell's presence became necessary for him.

"I wonder what she is doing?" he thought. He'd be probably surprised to learn that at the very same moment Isabella had exactly the same sort of discussion with her brother as he had with Lord Ravencroft.

"It's been more than two years since your husband's death," declared Haakon, "and I wish you to marry again. This time, I found you a marriage partner you probably won't object to. It's the new Duke of Argentson."

The princess turned deathly pale. "You must be kidding!"

"Do I look like it?" inquired Haakon. "I'm perfectly serious. He wanted the Duchy and he wanted you and he kept his end of the bargain. In about four months he's coming back to the capital and I want your engagement to be made public."

Isabella jumped to her feet and her eyes flashed. "Have I no say in the matter? Am I just a piece of merchandize for both of you? What if I refuse?"

The King rose up, too, and looked at his sister significantly. "It's either that or the convent, Bell. I won't have you living here unattached giving reason for people to gossip and for you to bring dishonor upon my name. Make your choice."

"I hate both of you," stated Isabella. "And will you please leave my room?"

"Will you please leave my room, Your Majesty. You have four months to think things over," declared her brother. "I hope you'll make a wise choice."

And so they parted.

Chapter 10. The Cardinal's Visit

The next three months were very long indeed. The finances of the province had been terribly mismanaged. The treasury was empty. Corruption reached the highest levels. The paperwork was a mess, the job market stagnant so that there were no jobs for young men. The palace of Eric's father was in ruins and thus, he had to share the residence of the late governor together with Lord Vernone and Derek White.

It was evident that Lord Hammerstone had used the Duchy as a cash cow and tried to squeeze as much as possible out of it. Rent was so high that small farmers were going bankrupt but no new projects were started. The roads hadn't been repaired, the electrical grid was dated. The part of the province which lay close to the border had a terrorist attack at least once a week. People were scared to openly show their loyalty to the new government.

The little industry that the Duchy had, was concentrated in the south and included some steel mills and the factories producing heavy machinery. Those were running more or less smoothly but their output was too small. Taxed to the maximum by the previous government, the owners lacked the means to modernize the equipment.

Eric met with them, promised lower taxes and suggested they'd start producing weapons for the needs of the state. The scheme proved successful and he was able to secure a loan from Haakon's government, part of which was then used as a one-time subsidy for the agricultural sector, while the rest went into rebuilding the infrastructure.

Lord Vernone worked overtime and so did Derek White as the joy of Eric's early successes was tempered by the fact that he had so far survived three attempts on his life: a bomb explosion at the market he was visiting, three gunmen waiting for his car on a lonely road and an assassin trying to cut his throat in his own bed.

Those behind the explosion found refuge across the border, the gunmen died in a shootout with Eric's security agents, but the hired assassin was caught alive and talked after being waterboarded and revealed some names. By this time, it was spring and only a week separated them from Easter holidays and His Eminence's visit. Both Derek White and Lord Vernone insisted that in order to provide his security and that of himself, Eric had to agree to drastic measures.

"I can't do it, really," he argued. "I can't put the province under de facto military rule. It won't make me more popular with common folks. Moreover, I'm not sure I agree with these methods. I can't sanction torture and extrajudicial executions."

"These methods work, Your Grace," said Lord Vernone earnestly. "You've seen it yourself in the case of that hired hitman. As for common folks, they are tired of constant terror threats. Most of them just want to live a normal life, without bombs going off when they least expect it."

"He's right, Eric," supported him Derek White. "Once in your life, listen to reason! Especially now. If something happens to Theodosius…"

"I'll think of it," promised Eric, "but I can't give you an answer right now. I need time to think it over! As for Theodosius, we must take all the necessary precautions to ensure that his visit runs smoothly. If this means more security staff and stricter safety measures I agree, but I'm not prepared to go any further at the moment."

His Eminence was planning to spend three days in Argentson, celebrate a liturgy in the main cathedral of its capital and address the people in the Artisian Square, right in front of the governor's palace. This intention of his was a source of constant headache to Eric from the security angle; even though he hoped that the cardinal would endorse his reign during this speech, he'd gladly do without allowing him to take such risks. He understood very well what a political disaster the death of Theodosius would be apart from the fact that he'd have to be right at the cardinal's side, too, during the occasion. The only thing the enemy needed, was a sniper rifle and a man with some training…

His Eminence's plane landed on time, without exploding in the air, and he reached the capital without any trouble. In his new role he became even more pompous and self-assured, but Eric checked himself and did his best to show him maximum hospitality. Theodosius appeared quite content, called Eric "my son" and hinted that if the latter chose to join One True Church they could be not just allies, but personal friends. Eric thought it fate worse than death and politely but firmly expressed his preferences for the religion of his fathers.

The cardinal smiled: "The rulers of Argentson have always been the loyal sons of One Church."

"He knows," thought Eric, but said aloud: "I can't change my creed because of political reasons alone. Faith is a matter of conscience as Your Eminence surely realizes. Unless I'm certain of my own beliefs I'll stick to…(he wanted to say 'the Devil I know' but stopped just in time) I'll stick to the religion I was baptized into. However, I'm perfectly ready to ensure free religious exercise for all my subjects."

They negotiated the matter for more than two hours and Eric congratulated himself with tricking the cardinal into thinking that he achieved more than Eric had originally planned to give. In fact, Theodosius went as far as suggesting to use church funds for the financing of the new cathedral project.

"May the blessings of Heaven rest upon Your Grace," he announced solemnly, "and my prayers will be that in time you'll be able to discern the truth and return to the manner of worship of your ancestors."

He obviously didn't dare to go further in his hints but Eric understood him perfectly well though he pretended that he hadn't.

The Easter sermon went fine. The old cathedral was full but no incident occurred. Eric started breathing more freely. One more day, and His Eminence would fly back home. Just one more day.

"God in Heaven," he prayed, "let nothing happen to the old fox. Let him return to Angharad safely."

In the meanwhile he discussed security measures with Derek White. Derek's men would check all the empty attics, interrogate every suspicious person coming into the proximity of the Artisian Square, patrol all the metro and train stations etc. etc.

The second Easter day dawned and the weather was exceptionally nice. It was quite warm and not a gray cloud in the sky. By 5 o'clock in the afternoon the square was full of people. Theodosius stood on a podium with Eric to the left of him and several security agents on both sides, partly covering them. Max, who was on duty today, stood right beside Eric.

An enormous TV screen was broadcasting the cardinal's speech so that every person present, no matter how far he stood, could hear him. He was truly at his best. His pompousness may have looked ridiculous at a dinner party, here in the open, addressing common folks, Theodosius had no equal.

He talked about the Easter message of resurrection and renewal and expressed the wish that the war-torn province would finally know peace. Eric hardly listened. He tried to appear interested but his eyes kept wandering, searching the crowds, scanning the roofs of the apartment buildings on the opposite side of the stage. Did he see something or was it just his imagination?

He had always had a good eyesight and for a second, he seemed to have caught a glimpse of the setting sun reflected in the telescopic visor of a sniper rifle. The very next moment he knew that he was not mistaken, though it was more his instinct than anything else. He hesitated only for a fraction of a second. Should Theodosius die, his own political career was finished, but it was not his ambition but rather his keen sense of responsibility which finally prompted him to act.

Eric jumped forward, so as to cover His Eminence, but he was too late as two things happened practically simultaneously: the TV screen above exploded in a blast of fire and a shadow, quick as a lightning, sprang in front of him, pushing both Eric and the cardinal to the ground.

"Max," he thought, and the last thing which his eyes registered was the image of Max convulsing as the sniper rifle rounds were tearing his chest apart. At that moment a heavy fragment of the screen hit him on his head and he fell on top of Theodosius and saw and heard no more.

Consciousness took its time returning, and with it, both pain and memory. When Eric finally came to his senses, he realized that he was lying in a hospital bed, with a doctor staying close by and Derek White holding his hand. His head was bandaged and it hurt like Hell but at that moment, there were two things only he cared about.

"Theodosius," he whispered coarsely and Derek smiled: "His Eminence is perfectly fine, Eric, which is a miracle in itself considering that you landed on top of him. He wants to see you and thank you as soon as possible."

Eric closed his eyes in quiet satisfaction and then opened them again. "And Max?"

"Your Grace," interrupted the doctor, "you have a heavy concussion, and you shouldn't talk too much. Drink some water and try to get some sleep."

"What happened to Max?" demanded Eric, this time speaking quite clearly.

"He's dead. I'm sorry," said Derek White. "The gunman is dead, too, if that's any consolation."

"I want to see Lord Vernone," announced Eric. "Immediately."

"Please, Major, don't let him exert himself too much, otherwise I can't answer for the consequences," interfered the doctor.

Derek shook his head. "You don't know how stubborn he is, Doctor Brown. However, he has a point. You'd better send someone to find His Lordship while I stay with him. I'll vouch for his good behavior."

Brown left and Eric closed his eyes and thought of Max and his young wife. "Marie, does she know?"

"She lost her child shortly afterwards. What are you planning to do now, Eric?"

"Something I should have done before," said the latter gloomily. "Something you and Lord Vernone told me I should have done."

Theodosius entered the hospital ward together with His Lordship. For the first time in his life he looked agitated and visibly shaken.

"You can't do it, Eric," he stated, forgetting all the formalities. "You can't restrict civil liberties in this manner. That's not the way. You can't drench the province in blood!"

"I can't, can I?" inquired Eric. "You bet I can! An eye for an eye and a tooth for a tooth sayeth the Scriptures, and for once I agree. Do you have the text of the decree with you, Lord Vernone?"

"Yes, my lord," answered the latter shoving it across the small side table together with a pen. Eric scanned the document and signed it.

"I'm sorry, Your Eminence, but this time they went too far. I want all responsible for this act of terror to hang!"

"I won't deny that you have your reasons for doing it," admitted the cardinal, "but I thought it my duty to express humanitarian concerns. However, the main reason I came here is to thank you for your noble gesture. I'm sorry about your bodyguard," and for once, he sounded perfectly sincere.

Eric suddenly felt awfully tired and dizzy. "If you could talk to his wife, Your Eminence…"

"I already did," answered Theodosius. "I'll leave you now as the doctor told me you need your rest. My prayers will always be with you, Your Grace."

"Thanks," muttered Eric sinking back onto his pillow. "And I wish you a safe flight back home."

Chapter 11. Courting Isn't Easy

Eric looked at his own reflection in the mirror and swore. The scar on his forehead, though partly concealed by his hair, cut his left brow in two and made his whole face look asymmetrical. It certainly didn't make him any more handsome. He knew it was a small price to pay since he had stayed alive, unlike his unfortunate bodyguard.

Eric ensured that the widow of Max would get an ample pension and trusted in the healing power of youth as the girl was hardly twenty yet. The doctor said there was no reason why she couldn't bear a child to term in future, should she marry again.

He himself had spent two weeks in hospital with Lord Vernone basically running the province in his absence and when he recovered, he found out that he had become quite popular with its inhabitants. Theodosius wasn't the only one to appreciate what he had called Eric's "noble gesture." Lord Hammerstone had gambled and lost this time, as he finally discovered that his supporters were abandoning his cause in the same way that rats would abandon a sinking ship.

Lord Vernone didn't abuse the power he was given but used it ruthlessly against those whom he perceived as an enemy and with the help of various "third degree" methods of interrogation Eric preferred to know nothing about soon neutralized the whole terrorist network operating in the capital.

The war was by no means over as the border areas were still giving them all a lot of trouble, but the things calmed down to such a degree that Eric had no qualms about leaving for a week to celebrate the King's birthday and the fact that his wife's pregnancy was just announced. It was by now the end of May and he was anticipating this visit which would include a meeting with his stepfather and Isabella. Derek White would accompany him while Lord Vernone stayed behind to manage the affairs of the Duchy.

Eric had heard from Haakon that the latter desired Eric's engagement to his sister to be made public, but he had also heard from another source that Isabella contemplated joining a convent.

"It's all my fault," he thought, remembering Lord Ravencroft's words. "I should have shown her more attention, but darn it, who could have thought that Bell would ever wish to become a nun! The whole idea is preposterous!"

Yet he had to admit to himself that deep down he had always been certain of Isabella's love and this fact and his wounded pride made him treat her in a manner bordering on insulting as he was pretty sure she would accept him in any case and that if her intention now was to cause him pain, she succeeded fully.

"And now, how am I supposed to court her, with a face like this?" he said aloud.

"You look fine," assured him Derek's voice behind his back. "Like a pirate or a highwayman. Women love it. It will get better with time, too."

"You are probably right," agreed Eric, "but it's still a bother."

"My God, you could have been decapitated by this screen, and you get upset because of a mere scratch!" said Derek, exasperated. "At least, now you'll have something to talk about when you meet each other. The whole court keeps discussing your unusual luck, Your Grace. It's the fourth assassination attempt you have survived so far."

"And probably not the last, as long as Hammerstone lives," responded Eric. "I wish we could do something about it. If he's destroyed, the whole insurrection movement will collapse on its own."

"I have thought of it, too," admitted Derek, "but it's difficult to penetrate his inner circle. And he has some powerful allies in the North, like the Lords of Lotar Mountains. That's where he's probably hiding at the moment. And they all support Uranius as one man, too. You can't solve this problem on your own, Eric. You need Haakon's help."

"I'll talk about it with the king," said Eric reluctantly.

"With him and with your father? He's been made the Chancellor of the Exchequer, as you know."

"With him and with Lord Ravencroft, yes," promised Eric.

Though the capital of the kingdom was Troon, Haakon decided to spend the summer in Angharad, the seat of his family's ancient power and the whole court moved together with him. Lord Ravencroft, the finance minister of the new government, returned to Raven's Nest, his country estate, and that's where he and his stepson met.

Raoul with his wife and two sons was also there so they had a family reunion of sorts. Eric's stepbrother, with his wife's family support, has become a successful businessman and started to express interest in politics, at least, at the local level. They met more cordially than Eric had expected as Raoul apparently didn't begrudge him his rise to power, but his step-brother's face darkened considerably when Lord Ravencroft stated that he wanted to talk to Eric alone.

"There is something I want to tell you," he started and Eric was just beginning to wonder whatever he had done wrong this time; when much to his surprise, Lord Ravencroft continued: "I have come to the conclusion that I wasn't completely fair to you, Eric. I misjudged your character and your motivation, and the recent incident with the cardinal proved it. The fact that you would sacrifice your life to save his, even though you don't have particularly friendly feelings towards the man, opened my eyes. I'm sorry."

Eric was so stunned that for a second he was unable to speak and Lord Ravencroft continued: "These last four months have been incredibly hard on you, I can see the reflection of what you've been through in your eyes. You carry a heavy responsibility but you have done well. I would be proud to call you my son and…you can count on my support should you need it."

"Thank you, sir," said Eric. "You have been the only…the only father I know. I appreciate your support."

They shook each other's hands and Eric laughed quietly. "You know, sir, it's probably the first time in my whole life that I have heard a word of approval out of your mouth."

"I was probably too strict," admitted Lord Ravencroft. "But you have always been so darn obstinate, even as a child. You were the only one in the whole household who dared contradict me. Anyway, let bygones be bygones. There are things in the present that demand our attention. What are you planning to do about the princess?"

"I'm going to propose to her," said Eric. "Tomorrow evening, at the party."

Haakon celebrated his 37th birthday with all the splendor his troubled budget allowed, his young queen by his side. It was already known she was carrying a son, one more reason for celebration. If one didn't take into consideration the fact that Freya was nearly twenty years his junior, they almost looked like a happy couple.

"And why not?" thought Eric. "His Majesty certainly can make a woman happy, if he takes the trouble."

And still he wondered if the king ever thought of Laura. There was a certain family likeness between the sisters, or was it only Eric's imagination? He looked around, talked to old acquaintances, greeted Theodosius who responded with some unusual cordiality and even found some time to discuss the border situation with Haakon, with the latter promising to send some of his own troops to guard the border and further financial support. With Eric's hands tied down by the troubled state of affairs in the Duchy he hardly represented a threat to the Royal Power anymore and so Haakon could afford to be generous.

Isabella was present, too, and when Eric finally met her and asked to dance with him, she accepted his invitation with a blush and a smile.

"We have been worried on your account, Your Grace," she stated quietly as Eric was leading her in a tour of waltz.

"Just call me Eric, will you?" he responded. "So you've been thinking about me while I was in exile?"

"Exile? Isn't it what you always wanted?" inquired the princess.

"It felt like an exile, without you!"

"Or without Laura?" she asked innocently.

"What has Laura to do with us?" retorted Eric curtly. "Why are you always dragging her into our conversations? Can't you just leave her alone?"

Isabella looked insulted for a moment, then a bitter smile appeared on her face. "It's just like I thought. You still love her."

"Nonsense," protested Eric. "I came here with one objective in my mind, to propose to you and you know it! Your brother told me."

"I'll never again marry a man who doesn't love me," declared the princess haughtily. "One time was enough. I'd rather join a convent."

"So it's true then," said Eric. "Well, if you prefer to spend the rest of your life with a bunch of silly women instead of me…"

"And they aren't silly!" exclaimed Isabella angrily and ran out through an open French window into the garden. Some of the people present looked at her with surprise and then saw Eric following her and nodded significantly and started whispering. He caught up with her by the tea house, grabbed her hand and forced her to go inside.

"Bell, listen to me, please! Let me explain! I do love you! I have loved you since the first time I saw you, long ago. Yes, I've had other women, but darn it, you couldn't expect me to live like a monk, could you? After all, you have been married yourself."

She turned away her head stubbornly and when he touched her cheek, he noticed she was crying and then he pulled her close to himself and started kissing her. Spring nights have a charm of their own and this one was not an exception as they both discovered that their mutual feelings were stronger than their common sense and all rules of decency.

It was a long night and when they finally fell asleep in each other's arms, the sky was already getting gray in the east. Eric slept soundly for a couple of hours but when he woke up he discovered that Isabella was gone. She left no message, no sign of her affection, nothing at all. In fact, the only proof that their encounter had really happened, was the sad state of his clothes.

He put them in some sort of order hastily, wondering if their disappearance had been noticed by many and at the same moment his mobile started ringing. It was Lord Vernone and his voice sounded dead serious: "Your Grace, you need to come back as soon as possible! We are dealing with the invasion from across the border right now. Have you talked to the King?"

"Yes, Lord Vernone, and he promised us military support. I'm going to him immediately and then I'm flying back. Hold on there."

Eric hang up and hurried to the Palace. He had to act quickly. As for Isabella, that matter could wait. He doubted very much that she would still desire to join any sort of convent after what had happened between them last night.

Chapter 12. How It All Ended

It was a sunny morning in mid-July and Eric was sitting in the garden of the governor's palace in the city of Argent, the capital of the Duchy of Argentson, with a cup of coffee in his hand, looking at the far-away Lotar Mountains. The snow on their tops didn't melt even in July sun.

Eric had all reasons to be content: the invaders were finally expelled and peace returned to the province, moreover, there were rumors going around that Lord Hammerstone had been found dead with a dagger through his heart; besides, today was Eric's 31st birthday and he had just received the keys to the new sports car he had bought a week before.

He had been working overtime, so he fully earned this one day of rest and could enjoy his morning coffee with a clear conscience. Eric was rather surprised when his butler appeared and announced that there was a lady who insisted on talking to him. After all, it was only 9 a.m.

"A lady?" inquired Eric. "What sort of a lady?"

"A fine lady, Your Grace. Very well dressed. She has red hair but her face is covered with a veil. She says she's an old acquaintance of Your Grace and something about the Queen of Elves."

"Let her in immediately, Jenkins," ordered Eric, jumping to his feet. "And bring one more coffee and see that no one disturbs us."

"Yes, Your Grace," said the butler shaking his head. He had never seen his master so agitated before.

This time Laura was wearing a smart dark blue suit with a rather short skirt and a small hat with a short veil, which she removed as she gingerly seated herself across the table.

"Thank you," she said accepting a cup of coffee from Jenkins, then smiled and stared at Eric's face for a moment: "That must have hurt."

"Not really," he lied. "You may go, Jenkins. What an unexpected pleasure," he continued when they were finally left alone. "What's new across the border?"

"Lord Hammerstone is dead."

"I've heard the story, but is it certain?"

"I saw him die," said Laura significantly.

Eric looked at her, stunned: "Was it you who killed him?"

Laura laughed. "You don't expect me to answer that question, do you? By the way, you have greetings from a couple of old acquaintances."

"I have no acquaintances in Lotar," said Eric, even more surprised.

"I spent the last week or so on Aargh," explained Laura. "One Alec Randall sends you his best wishes and something else, too." She opened her handbag and took a small file out of it. "Here's your Deltan passport, Your Grace. You never know when you will need it."

Eric took the file in his hands and examined the contents for some time, then looked back at Laura. "Well, that kinda brings things into perspective a bit, doesn't it? And my second acquaintance?"

"A wealthy young widow whose maiden name used to be Irene Stedler expressed a lot of interest in your fate. She was even making plans as to visit Dakstra in the future."

"God forbid," stated Eric and they both laughed.

They spent a couple of hours together talking about old acquaintances and Eric showed her the palace and even discussed with her the renovation plans for different parts of it. He made the drawings himself in his spare time and was quite proud of the fact.

"I still could earn my bread as an architect, should the need arise," he declared. "And what are you planning to do now?"

"I'll return to Aargh, and then we'll see," responded Laura. "By the way, it's your birthday today, isn't it? Alec told me. You've got a present from me but it's surely not the only one?"

"No, of course not. I have a new sports car which was just delivered here this morning. Actually, Jenkins brought it and handed over the keys right before you turned up. Come on, I'll show you."

He took her to the parking lot beneath the windows of his own apartment.

"Which garage does it come from?" inquired Laura.

"The new one down town, it was recommended to me by the butler."

"Jenkins? Did I tell you that his face looks familiar to me. He doesn't work here very long, does he? Now, can I try driving it first? You know I adore fast cars!"

She took the keys out of Eric's hand and jumped in. Her words produced a strange impression on Eric who suddenly felt that it was very important to remember under which circumstances Jenkins had got his job. Laura installed herself in the driver's seat and her hand touched the ignition key. A horrible suspicion flashed through Eric's mind.

"Laura, no!!! Don't do it!!!" But it was too late.

The force of the explosion was such that the glass of all the windows on the first floor was shattered and Eric was thrown hard against the palace wall and lost his consciousness for some time, but when he came to the first thing which he saw were the flames engulfing what was left of his new car and of Laura.

Ten days later Derek White entered Lord Vernone's office. "You wanted to see me, your Lordship?" he asked.

"How is he?" inquired Lord Vernone instead of an answer.

Derek shook his head. "Physically he is OK, but mentally…The worst thing is that he keeps blaming himself for what has happened."

"Did you try to talk to him, Major?"

"I did, but he won't listen. The doctors say that's a normal psychological reaction to the shock, but sometimes I'm afraid…"

Derek didn't finish his sentence as at that moment there was some noise behind the door and a shrill female voice said: "Let me in, immediately. I have something of utmost importance to communicate."

At that very moment Eric was sitting all alone in his own office behind the writing desk. He pulled out a drawer and took out a ray gun. The weapon felt heavy in his hand. With a click the safety mechanism got disengaged. Now what was the best manner to shoot oneself? Through the temple or through the mouth?

He felt strangely detached, as if it all was happening to someone else. The only thing he had to do now was to pull the trigger and then his misery would be over. Or wouldn't it? Didn't religion teach that suicide was a mortal sin? But he had no religion or did he? It all appeared so complicated.

"No, you can't do it," said a voice in his head. "You can't run away from your responsibilities. Not in this manner. That's an act of cowardice."

"My responsibilities weigh too heavy on my shoulders," he protested. "I can't carry them alone."

"You aren't alone," responded the voice. "You have friends and family. And God is always with you."

"Then why did He take away those who were dearest to me? Why, Lord, why? All my friends die one after another and I'm left to live."

"Because you are a destiny child," came the answer. "You have a mission to fulfill. And you won't resurrect your friends by your desertion, either."

"Our Father which art in Heaven, Hallowed be Thy name, Thy will be done," whispered Eric, then sighed, put the safety pin back in its initial position and was just going to place the pistol back into the drawer when the door suddenly swung open and Isabella rushed in. She had persuaded Derek White to give her the spare key as she was feeling that the urgency of the situation demanded it. She looked rather tired, with dark circles under her eyes.

"Put that thing down," she screamed, with a horrified expression on her face. "You can't do it! Not now, when…"

She didn't finish the sentence as her face turned deathly pale and she would have fainted had Eric not hurried to her rescue. He seated her into a chair, brought her a glass of water and, after closing and locking the drawer asked sympathetically: "Feeling any better?" Isabella nodded.

"How on Earth could you think I was going to kill myself? And what did you mean when you said I couldn't do it now?"

She raised her eyes and lowered them again. "Was I mistaken?"

"No," admitted Eric reluctantly. "I did want an easy way out but now I realize I could have never done it. I can't just quit. It would mean that the sacrifice of others were in vain." And he thought of Andy Shultz and Max Lain and Laura and all the rest. They were both silent for a moment, then Eric continued: "But you still owe me an explanation. First of all, how did you come here? I haven't heard from you since…since that night."

"I haven't heard from you, either."

"But I had an invasion to deal with and then…" He didn't finish his sentence.

The princess looked at him. "I wanted to tell you, Eric, that I'm sorry, really sorry. I wish I could change it. You loved her so…"

Eric shook his head. "Our affair was over, Bell. We both knew and accepted it. Those feelings turned into something else. Regard, friendship. I don't know…"

"Then why did you want to die?" she inquired.

"Because I felt myself responsible for what had happened. It was just too much for me at the moment. But then I realized it was a cowardly thing to do…Well, let's not talk about it anymore. Tell me about yourself. What's new?"

Isabella suddenly blushed and Eric looked at her with more attention. Those dark circles, this fainting fit…Could it be..?

"Bell, why did you come?"

"Because I had to tell you something…can't you guess what?" she whispered.

"Just tell me what it is!"

"Well, if you insist…you are going to become a father!"

"Congratulations," said Derek's voice behind her back. "Now you two will finally have to marry each other!"

"Eavesdropping should be a capital offence," retorted Eric but he didn't sound at all angry.

They were married in a brief ceremony a week later, and much to Theodosius's disappointment, Isabella accepted her husband's religion. They called their firstborn son Eric, in honor of his father, but when they got a daughter one and a half year later, it was Isabella who insisted on her being called Laura.

And here the story ends, but whether they lived long and happily ever after is the subject of another book.

The End.

www.ingramcontent.com/pod-product-compliance
Lightning Source LLC
Chambersburg PA
CBHW021011180626
46814CB00003B/1250